TIMOTHY FINDLEY

STONES

VIKING

VIKING
Published by the Penguin Group
Penguin Books Canada Ltd, 2801 John Street, Markham,
Ontario, Canada L3R 1B4
Penguin Books Ltd, 27 Wrights Lane, London W8 5TZ, England
Viking Penguin Inc., 40 West 23rd Street, New York,
New York 10010, USA
Penguin Books Australia Ltd, Ringwood, Victoria, Australia
Penguin Books (NZ) Ltd, 182-190 Wairau Road, Auckland 10,
New Zealand
Penguin Books Ltd, Registered Offices: Harmondsworth,
Middlesex, England

First published 1988

1 3 5 7 9 10 8 6 4 2

Copyright © Pebble Productions Inc., 1988

Printed and bound in Canada

Canadian Cataloguing in Publication Data

Findley, Timothy, 1930-
Stones

ISBN 0-670-82297-3

I. Title.

PS8511.I573S76   1988   C813'.54   C88-094749-7
PR9199.3.F548S76   1988

The information on page vi constitutes an extension
of the copyright page.

For

Michael

and in memory of

Sal

We are tomorrow's past.

Mary Webb

"Bragg and Minna" first published in the *Malahat Review*, Fall 1987;
"Foxes" first published in *Rotunda*, Summer 1987;
"The Name's the Same" first published in *Grain*, Spring 1987;
"Almeyer's Mother" first published in *Saturday Night*, June, 1988.

Extracts of "Goodbye Yellow Brick Road"
by Elton John and Bernie Taupin.
Courtesy of Elton John/Bernie Taupin, and Dick James Music Ltd.
All rights reserved.

"Resume" by Dorothy Parker
From *The Portable Dorothy Parker*
Copyright 1926, renewed © 1954 by Dorothy Parker
Reprinted by permission of Viking Penguin Inc.,
and
From *Dorothy Parker*
Reprinted by permission of Gerald Duckworth

CONTENTS

STONES

BRAGG AND MINNA

For Charlotte Engel

This is what Minna had written before she died:

Bragg always said we shouldn't have the baby and every-thing was done a man can do to prevent it. Still, I wanted her and she was born and now I realize I've given birth to all of Bragg's worst fears.

Bragg could see himself walking with the others up the hill — whatever the hill was called — the hill that led to Ku-Ring-Gai. He could see the three men walking upwards and the other two, the man and the woman, waiting on the level where the car was parked. He could see all this with perfect recall — staring down from the Plexiglas window, riding in the 747 high above the Pacific Ocean. All he had to do in order to regain the scene on the hill — or any scene — was turn the memory projector on in his mind and run the film: three men walking up the hill to Ku-Ring-Gai — himself; his lover, Col; and Nob, the sad, mad poet from Sydney who was their guide that afternoon.

The day he was scanning — which was yesterday — had been humid, hot and dusty and the air had been thick with the sound of feeding insects. For whatever reason, the insects themselves could not be seen and Bragg — so appallingly tense to begin with — had begun to extract from their invisibility the sort of menace endured by the blind. He kept on trying to brush the sound of them away from his eyes and he dared not speak for fear he would swallow something deadly.

Everything had gone awry....

(Now, that's a nice old-fashioned phrase, my dear; he thought — in Minna's voice:

> There I was, so hot and dry
> and everything had gone awry....)

Still, it was true. All or any hope that some happy trace of Minna would emerge from his search had faded completely. What he had wanted was a sign — a signal that he could lay her ghost to rest at Ku-Ring-Gai without a sense of despair. But no such signs or signals had been forthcoming. On the other hand, his search for *Minna memori* had not been without its clues that she had definitely passed that way before him. The signs of her passage had been unmistakable: the red wine spilled on all the rugs, the dirty jokes repeated with all their Minna-twists-and-turns, the

4

dark brown trail of cigarette butts and burns as plain as the bread crumbs scattered by Hansel and Gretel when they entered the deadly wood. So Bragg could say: "I certainly know she's been here" — but all he got in reply was a nod without elaboration. The trouble was that everyone Bragg had interviewed had wanted to protect him from the truth — they didn't want to be the first to spill the beans: as if he didn't know the beans were in the pot.

All this, of course, was part of the usual Minna Joyce conspiracy; the network of spies and allies set up everywhere she went. Long ago Bragg had said that if Minna had chosen to go down into the Antarctic, she could have established a successful branch of the Minna Joyce conspiracy amongst the King penguins. Such was the power of her belief in who she was and in everything she did, no matter the consequence.

Damn the consequence! That was her motto. And damn the mayhem she brought wherever she went and damn the anguish she left behind whenever she went away.

So, now he was carrying Minna's ashes up the hill to Ku-Ring-Gai....

He was watching Nob, "the sad, mad poet from Sydney" (that was a quote from one of Minna's letters), struggling up the path before him, bleeding his gin-soaked perspiration into his dark green shirt. He wondered what it was that Stanley Nob — so undeniably sad, but maybe not so mad — had known about Minna? What had they shared that Nob was refusing to share with Bragg? Had they slept so happily together...? Did he sleep with everyone he met, the way that Minna had? Bragg could so easily make the picture of it: Nob was so damned good looking...Bragg had wanted him himself. But the picture of himself with Nob was not the picture Bragg was making climbing up the hill.

5

The picture he was making had to do with desperation: maybe the very picture of desperation itself. It was of Nob and Minna sweating — bathed in their mutual sorrow — struggling the way she had struggled with him, with Bragg, against his refusal to give her a child: struggling in behalf of her own determination that he would. *Come on and fuck, you bastard!* she had told him — yelling at him. *Don't you understand? If we don't fuck, we die.*

If we don't fuck, we die.

Another nice old-fashioned phrase, my dear.

Had she known, even then, that she was dying — or was it just the babble of someone driving someone else to climax?

On the hill, Bragg shut his eyes because he didn't want to look any more at Nob's sweating back. It told him the one sure thing he didn't want to know: that Minna had escaped him utterly.

On the plane — which was taking them to San Francisco — there was a washed-out, brazen girl who looked like Janis Joplin. She was wandering up and down the aisles, claiming she was alone but treating all the passengers as if they were her relatives and friends. Bragg could see she was almost totally gone on something — more than likely cocaine — and she kept augmenting whatever it was with swigs of whisky from a so-called can of beer.

Bragg had seen her fill the beer can earlier from a bottle of Chivas Regal she kept amongst some clothing in her bag. The bag was one of those shapeless, woven things they sell in every market-place from Marrakesh to Lima — its colours bleached and blotched from infusions of too much sun and too much dye. When the girl sat down beside him, shaking out her brown frizzy hair, Bragg could smell a whole biography of odours rising from the lumpy shape in her lap: of suntan lotion, hash oil, bourbon and expensive perfume. He noticed the girl held onto the bag as if it were alive and he also noticed that her fingernails were chewed.

"Hey," she said — lifting her black-rimmed Foster Grants high enough for Bragg to see her eyes — "am I sitting here?" She squinted at him, smiling and ingratiating — wincing at the light. Her eyes were like two cracked marbles that might have been green.

"You may be sitting here now," Bragg said, "but not when my friend comes back."

"Oh," the girl said. "You're not alone. Dammit." She seemed to be genuinely disappointed.

"That's right," Bragg told her. "My friend has gone to the washroom."

"You mean he's gone to the head," she said. "On a plane they call it the head. The same as on a ship...."

"I always call it the washroom."

"Oh, the *wash* room," the girl said — making fun of him. "Oh, the *wash* room!" she said. "I have to go to the *wash* room!" She laughed and took another swig from her beer can.

Bragg looked away from her and sat still. He hoped that Col would come back soon and make the girl move on. It wasn't just that she was becoming obnoxious. Bragg could deal with that; he'd certainly had the requisite training. But the girl was beginning to remind him of Minna — the husky voice that wandered up and down the scale — the smell of her perfume, which he knew by now was Opium — and the stench of alcohol. It was unbearable.

Then the girl said: "You know what, mister? You look awful sad. Like someone died."

Bragg didn't utter.

"Me, I'm not allowed to look sad," the girl informed him, trying not to smile. "I'm not allowed to look sad, cause I'm going home now, to be married. In San Francisco." She was silent for a moment and Bragg turned to look at her and then she said: "Is this a smoking section we're sitting in?"

He held up his cigarette so the Janis Joplin girl could see it burning. Now she's going to ask me for one; he thought — and then she'll come back and back and back and ask me over and over for more cigarettes — all the way to San Francisco. That's how she'll trap me. That's how she'll bond me to her: just the way Minna did. And next thing I know, I'll be lifting her luggage off the carousel — arranging for her cab and making sure she gets to her hotel.

"You got a cigarette?" she asked.

"No," said Bragg. "I haven't. I'm smoking my very last one."

"Oh," the girl said, and she laughed out loud. "You expecting a firing squad or something?" She got up slowly then and went away from him down the aisle.

There was a great solid plain of clouds below them now above the sea, and Bragg could not imagine where they were. The Janis Joplin girl had wandered off in search of another vacant seat — and Bragg had watched her pausing here and there to stare down into someone's face and asking them: "should I be sitting here?" — then moving on. Squinting, he could turn her all too easily into Minna and he could all too easily imagine Minna doing the same thing, re-arranging the passengers to suit herself — except that

8

Minna would have phrased her injunction differently. Minna would have said: "I can't imagine how this has happened…" smiling, charming, poised for the punch line: "but you're sitting in my seat…" blowing smoke in her victim's face — "and you'll have to move your ass."

Or, if she was working in her lady-mode: "I wonder if you'd mind…?" And then: "of course, I can have you forcibly removed…."

And she would have had the baby with her; carrying the child for all the world to see on her hip. Minna with Stella, running all the way to Australia, just to escape from Bragg and die in peace.

Or, so he believed.

Colin Marsh and Stuart Bragg had met in Toronto before Bragg's marriage to Minna went on the rocks. But Colin had nothing to do with driving them apart; that was all internal, deep inside the marriage itself and, indeed, so deep that even Bragg and Minna, with all the help of all the psychoanalysts in all the world would not have known where to look for the fissures. Some people seek each other out — Col remembered being told — in order to complete a circle. But what we have not been told is that, sometimes the circle being completed is a kind of death trap. We have not been told some people seek each other out in order to be destroyed.

Now, when Col came back they ordered drinks but were otherwise silent. Col was good at feeling out a silence. He could tell, before he put his hands out, where the snakes were going to be.

We are told, Col thought, as he looked at his friend beside him, an awful pack of lies about love. Some big cheese in everyone's life is always handing down some line about people being made for each other, as if the violins would always play: as if Anne Murray would always sing at all the anniversaries. The truth was, no one sang. The only example Col had ever had of anyone getting all the way through to the end intact had been his parents — and they had so many secrets from one another, it had only been their lies that kept them together.

Col looked away and began to scan the covers of the books being read around him. He wondered if any of the books were Bragg's — or Minna's. It was always the strangest feeling when that happened; when he saw, with a start, the cover of one of Bragg's or Minna's books. Strangers, it seemed, were invading his private world — the world at home where the books were written and Bragg leaned over his pages, looking like a giant bug — a beetle by lamplight.

Bragg's room was upstairs — his cabinet, as he liked to call it — though it hadn't any door, but only a curtain. Col used to go up late at night to see if Bragg was ready to go to bed — but the back beneath the lamplight and the cigarette smoke that curled up past the green glass shade were all the signal he needed to go away. Col slept halfway down the hall in a room between Bragg's cabinet and Minna's bedroom. Bragg slept sometimes with one and sometimes the other. Sometimes, he slept in the sunroom — bunched on the wicker couch with Ben, his dog. This was in the house on Collier Street — not the one they lived in now, on Binscarth up in north Rosedale. Minna had refused to live in Rosedale. "Them as live in Rosedale," Minna had said to Col, in her tea-time imitation of Eliza Doolittle, "are them as keep their shit in jars."

My dear.

Col smiled even now, as he thought of Minna's hatred for

what she called *ladyhood*. She saw it as the enemy of everything she wanted women to be. It had almost destroyed her — or so she claimed — brought up the way she was, with "a silver spoon in every orifice...." Not that getting rid of them was easy. Minna's life, until she met Bragg and married him, had been a life of inherited privilege mixed with deliberate squalor. She'd gone to live in Parkdale, "my dear — with all its resident rubbies and gentle crazies, dressed in all weathers in their summer coats and woollen mittens and all their hair cut straight across in bangs and all with their tam-o'-shanters pulled down over their ears and their eyes as crafty and innocent all at once as the eyes of bears...." She used to talk like that to Col, when they sat together over her bottles of Côtes-du-Rhône in the kitchen late at night. And she would wave her cigarette as she talked, weaving her images out of smoke, and her voice was hoarse, and Col had definitely fallen in love with her, though not the way Bragg had fallen in love — not fiercely, as if to be in love was to call up all your anger — but in love the way all men were in love with the made-up women in their minds: those women who never get a chance to come down into the streets and walk around real because once they were real, like Minna, they threw you off balance and blew you away. A boy like Col could be in love with such a woman because he never had to contend with her needs. He only had to watch and listen and pay attention and pour the wine. And Col could do this by the hour.

She told him — more or less in the voice with which she wrote — of how she had moved into Parkdale out of Rosedale after her mother and father had been divorced and each one wanted her to live with them "and do good works." Like marry Harry Connacher and raise two dozen kids — (her mother's version of a good work) — or "use that brain

11

of yours to conquer the real-estate world" — (her father's version). Minna's version of a good work had been to go and live among the poor — "not only the poor in pocket, but the poor who were in pain and maddened by the same confusion that tampered with me. And you know" — and here, she had burst out laughing — "you know what I discovered? Half the people I was consorting with on Queen Street were *artists*! Artists and actors and poets and playwrights! Novelists, like Bragg. And, oh my God, it suddenly occurred to me that — looking out from the very same pain and madness — the only difference between the schizoids and the artists was articulation. And when I realized that what I had was articulation, I started to write like someone possessed — because I saw so clearly that I had found—*don't laugh* — but I had found, at last, a true good work that I could do with all my heart." Here, Minna sat back and drank a great, long draft of Côtes-du-Rhône and made a kind of doodle on the oilcloth with her fingernail. And when she spoke again, she spoke almost shyly:

"I figure that's the one and maybe the only thing my mom and dad were right about, Col. The doing of good works. It only depends on what a good work is. For me, it's putting an end to all the silence out on Queen Street. It's putting words where no words are and giving articulation to all that noise behind those eyes I'd been watching, innocent and crafty as a bear's...." Then she had looked up and said: "you understand what I'm saying, here?"

Col had said "yes" — that he understood. And, of course, that was precisely what Minna had done with her books: she had given articulation to "all that noise."

Minna's office on Collier Street had been the dining-room

and it had french doors with dozens of panes of glass she had painted over with white enamel. No one was allowed inside and she had kept it locked whenever she was working. Given her love of wine and people, Minna had almost phenomenal discipline and she produced much more than Bragg. Bragg was a slow and careful writer, and his books, which some considered to be very, very fine, were rather like etchings on brass over which he laboured long and achingly and hard. One of his favourite quotations came from Flaubert, who said: *I spent the morning putting in a comma — and the afternoon taking it out.* Bragg really did do that. He could spend the whole day writing a single sentence and tear it up before he went to bed. He produced his books at three-year intervals — all of them short and terse — and there were five of them, going on six — the sixth being written, but not to be published until the coming fall. Minna had written eleven books before she died — and there were four in bureau drawers. Not that she'd written with any less care than Bragg, but she'd had a good deal more to tell — and she'd told it with less ambiguity. And this was very much the way she had lived.

Bragg saw that Col had fallen asleep and after he'd ordered a second drink, he tried to sit back and relax. But he couldn't make himself comfortable. The seats had not been made for human beings.

His mind flew around the plane like a bird not knowing where to land. As always, it wanted to avoid the subject of Minna but no matter where it perched, she turned up — somehow — under its claws.

The baby. That was the final bone of contention and the birth of the child had driven them apart.

Bragg had never wanted children. He didn't trust his genes. He even had a theory that "maybe I'm a genetic homosexual." This theory was that, since there had been genetic defects in other generations of his family — clubbed feet — cleft palates — mongoloid children — mental illness — maybe his genes were calling a halt. Maybe his genes were saying: *no more babies.*

Ergo: "what better way than to create a homosexual?"

Minna had stared at him — at first in amusement, then in horror.

"You know who you sound like, don't you? I mean — I trust you know exactly who this sounds like, standing here talking in our living-room on Collier Street?"

Bragg gave two or three blinks — his way of trying to call up words when the words wouldn't come.

"No," he said. "I don't know who it sounds like."

"Hitler," said Minna. "Adolf Fucking Hitler!"

She took an explosive drag on her cigarette and almost drowned herself in wine by drinking it too quickly.

Bragg was amazed and confused all at once.

"I don't think I quite understand," he said. "You mean that because I think I may be a genetic homosexual, that makes me like Adolf Hitler?"

"Yes!" she shouted.

Bragg sat down.

"You'll have to explain," he said. "I'm not quite up to this."

"You've heard, I trust, of the Master Race?"

"Of course I have."

"Well — think about it! Think what Hitler was willing to do in order to achieve it. Think what he *did*! My dear, he would have loved it if you'd come along and spouted your genetic homosexual nonsense." She looked at him and

14

leaned down into his face before she spoke again. "You're playing right into his hands, Bragg! You're playing right into the hands of every goddamned maniac who thinks he can line up the human race and cull it by its genes. Blue eyes here and brown eyes over there!"

"It was only a theory, Minna. You don't have to get so excited."

"YOU ARE NOT A GENETIC HOMOSEXUAL, GOD DAMN IT! THERE IS NO SUCH THING AS A GENETIC HOMOSEXUAL!"

She stood in the middle of the room and virtually screamed this at him.

It frightened him.

Didn't she understand? He was trying to save her from giving birth to monsters.

"MAYBE WHAT I WANT IS MONSTERS!" she yelled.

Bragg could believe this.

Then she said — very quietly — folding her hands before her: "at least the monsters would be ours." And when she lifted her head, she was crying.

Bragg stood up and put his arms around her and took her back to the sofa where he poured her another glass of wine and held out her box of cigarettes and sat down beside her.

"I'm frightened," he said. "I can't have children."

Minna sniffed and blew her nose half-heartedly on a wad of yellow Facelle she'd found behind the pillows.

"I'll kick Col out of the house," she told him. "I'll kick Col out of the house and I'll cut your balls off...."

Good. She was laughing.

But she wasn't laughing. She was crying again and trying to speak:

"I'm thirty-eight years old," she said. "In another year it

15

will be too late. I love you, Bragg, and you love me. The only thing that matters, having children, is that those who have them love one another...."

"Oh, come off it," Bragg said. "Don't pull that one on me. Adolf Hitler's parents loved one another."

"But I want a baby."

"Have one. Be my guest."

"You bastard! How dare you say that? I don't want anyone's baby. I want yours. I want yours. I want it to be ours."

"I'm sorry," said Bragg. "I really am sorry. The answer is no."

They sat there — holding one another's hands — sipping their wine and smoking their cigarettes, each one plotting through the twilight how they would thwart the other.

In the long run, Minna won.

Stella was born on a rainy day in autumn.

Bragg took Minna down to the Wellesley Hospital and he and Col sat out in the waiting room. Col read magazines. Bragg went mad.

Minna was in labour twenty-two hours. At one point, the doctor came and asked Bragg's permission to administer an anaesthetic. Minna had refused it — but the pain was terrible.

Bragg said: no — that if Minna wanted the anaesthetic she would ask for it. She knew what she was doing and she hadn't wanted drugs and she hadn't wanted Bragg to be in the delivery room. Everything was being done the way she wanted it and Bragg was not going to interfere.

"I'm sorry," said the doctor. "She's really in very bad and quite unnecessary pain." And then he went away.

Two hours later, he came back into the room.

Bragg didn't have to ask. He was sure that Minna was dead. Either Minna was dead or the child was dead; or both. The doctor's face was full of all this possible information.

"Your wife will be fine," the doctor said. "She had a very bad time, but she'll be fine. She's a strong, resilient woman."

Suddenly, the doctor sat down in one of the leather chairs. He pushed back his surgeon's cap and did the unthinkable: he lighted a cigarette. He noticed both Col and Bragg had watched him do this in disbelief. He smiled and waved the cigarette in the air and said to them brightly: "I also drink and drive."

Bragg, who had been standing, sat down. Col went over to the window and watched the rain.

"I'm waiting for the bad news, doctor," said Bragg. "It's obvious you've come to tell me something has gone wrong. The child," he said, "is the child alive?"

"Yes," said the doctor. "The child is alive. You have a girl — and your wife has already said she wants to call her Stella."

"That means star," said Col.

"Indeed, sir. Yes — it does. Stella means star."

The doctor sat far back in his chair and put both his hands on its arms. He began to pick obsessively at the leather under his right thumb.

"Well?" said Bragg.

The doctor took a drag on his cigarette and regarded what his thumb nail had accomplished in terms of wrecking the arm of the chair. "Your daughter…" he began. "Stella…"

"Yes?"

"She has six fingers on each hand. She has six toes on each foot."

Bragg lay back against the sofa — stared at the ceiling and put his hand across his mouth. He didn't utter a word.

17

After a moment, the doctor stood up and crushed his cigarette underfoot. Then he said: "I'm afraid that isn't all."

Bragg crouched and waited.

Col was wishing that he hadn't come.

"There's brain damage, too. Not anyone's fault. Just one of those things a person can't foresee. I warned your wife..."

"I warned her, too," said Bragg.

But the doctor didn't seem to hear him. He went right on talking. "There's always a danger with the mother past the age of thirty-five. I told her that — warned her. But — " He threw up his empty hands. " — who listens any longer?" Then he said: "I repeat. She's a strong, resilient woman and she will recover."

"What about the baby?" Bragg asked. "Will the baby recover?"

"Stella," the doctor informed him, "will not recover. Of course she will not recover. No one with half a brain can recover, Mister Bragg. Your daughter, I'm afraid, is doomed. I'm sorry."

Before he left, the doctor turned at the door and said: "You can come and see me any time you want — but not today. I've just spent thirty-six hours on my feet and I'm going home, now, to die."

He was gone.

Col said: "what can I do for you?"

Bragg said: "you can take me home and let me screw you to the wall."

Later on, Bragg went into the ravine along Rosedale Valley Road and he walked in the mud. Coming to an open space, he found a fallen tree and he sat in the rain and let the weather have its way.

Six months later, Minna discovered she had inoperable cancer of the lung.

She hung around the house for several days and played with Stella. Bragg said nothing. He'd hardly said a word since Stella was born. All he did was pretend to write.

Finally, Minna came up the stairs one day — it was early summer now — and she was carrying Stella the way she always did, against her hip.

"I'm going to leave you, Bragg," she said.

Bragg set down his pen and put one hand against his temple to support his head. With the other hand, he turned out the lamp.

He sat on the bed and watched her for what seemed hours while she packed. He memorized her face and the way she moved and he memorized her smell.

"Where in Australia?" he asked her.

"I don't know. I've never been there. Probably Sydney. They say it's really quite civilized."

"Go where the doctors are good — that's all that matters," he said. "Just be sure you end up somewhere where the doctors are good."

"Soon as I know where we're going to be, I'll write."

"What about Stella — after you...?"

"Die? Not to worry. I'm determined I'm going to find her somebody desperate as me to love her and I'll leave her there."

Bragg could only think that Minna was crazy: mad. How could a sane person speak so blithely of "finding somebody desperate as me" to take in a child who was doomed to be a baby all her life? He wanted to yell at her; forbid her to go. He wanted to turn the police and the courts and ten thousand social workers onto her case and have her restrained. But how could a man do that to someone like Minna? All Minna wanted was to do good works in love.

In the long run — judging from the myriad of sources stamped on all her cards and letters — Minna had taken the whole of Australia to be her safe, good place: *almost as rewarding,* as she wrote to Col, *as taking up residence in Parkdale.*

She was a faithful, if somewhat spotty correspondent. Weeks could go by without a word. She was in Brisbane; she was in Cairns; she was in Adelaide; she was in Perth. At the end, she was in Sydney. And in all these places, she walked with Stella on her hip and in all these places she made what she herself called a raft of friends, though none — as she confessed to Bragg — as desperate as she for Stella's love. Still, this did not deter her. Right until the very last month, she was on her feet and walking.

One time, she wrote to Bragg and said: *I wonder if I ever told you why I called her Stella. Not for the sky-stars, my dear, but for the stars she holds in her fists: the six-pointed stars of Stella's hands.*

Another time, she wrote and said: *six fingers bad — five fingers good. That ring a bell? Get out your* Animal Farm *and read. We've been bamboozled far too long into accepting there can be no acceptance for those of us with four legs.*

Finally, she wrote and said: *I may have them here in Sydney. Childless as you and me for all those years — and they love her, Bragg. Their names are Viv and Charlie Roeback — comfortable as two old shoes. Charlie looks like Sidney Green-*

street playing Doctor Johnson. Viv looks like a mountain moved by faith. And they love her, Bragg. They love her…

Thank God, however, they did not — apparently — love her desperately. So, at least, they appeared to be realists.

It was only in the last of all the letters, written just before the cancer and its necessary regimen of heavy, incapacitating drugs finally forced her to lay down her pen, that Minna mentioned Nob — *the sad, mad poet of Sydney* — with whom she had shared a house before she went into the hospital to die. *He's a great, tall, crazy man who spent some time in an asylum for depression,* she wrote. *Just my type. Tell Col he writes about the noises in behind the eyes of bears; he'll understand. I'll always love you, Bragg — but I love this man a little, too. I'm even going to be cruel enough to say — because I have to, don't I, tell the truth? Crazy Stan Nob would have given me a dozen babies — drop of a hat, Bragg. Drop of a hat. Farewell.*

And that was all.

The next letter came from Viv and Charlie Roeback, saying that Minna was dead and they had Stella, safe and sound.

When they got to Sydney, it was Charlie Roeback who met them. Bragg had never seen a man so large. It required, in the restaurant, two chairs side by side to hold him.

Bragg and Col had come down slowly from Cairns to Brisbane to Sydney, taking their time to seek out all those others Minna had cultivated: the Minna Joyce Conspiracy. They also took the time to stare at the hordes of rosella birds and cockatoos and cockatiels and the wading ibis and the jabirus and the tiny, crazy peaceful doves, no longer than a box of cigarettes. In a zoo, when they saw a

21

duck-billed platypus, Col remained silent. All he could think of was Minna, shouting at Bragg in the living-room below him: *MAYBE I WANT TO GIVE BIRTH TO MONSTERS!*

And now they were in Sydney, where they had come to say goodbye to Stella and to scatter Minna's ashes on the heights at Ku-Ring-Gai.

Bragg, in the aeroplane above the Pacific, approaching San Francisco, turned on the memory projector again in his mind and rolled the film.

Three men walking up the hill, and down at the bottom Viv and Charlie Roeback waiting by the car with Stella lying in the shade.

Stanley Nob's sweating green back had reached the top and he was turning this way and that with shaded eyes to see where they must go.

Bragg, arriving out of breath, could hardly stand up straight he was so out of shape. He clutched the box of Minna's ashes to his breast and patted it reassuringly several times. "It's all right, now," he said. "We're here."

Stretching out before them and receding through the shimmering dust and heat, a great plateau of rock surrounded them on every side. Stone waves rolled beneath them, dizzy-making if you looked too far afield.

"I think," said Nob, "it's over that way where she wants to be scattered." And he began to walk away from them, making for a place unseen beyond the low-lying scrub that was everywhere in evidence.

Bragg and Col set out to follow him, but almost at once, Col stopped in his tracks and pointed down at the rocks.

"Look," he said. "Petroglyphs."

And, indeed, there were. Rock carvings — deep incisions

— God knew how old, of beasts and fish and birds.

And men.

"What are these, Nob?" Col asked.

Nob called back: "the Aborigines put them there. We don't really know just when — but long before the white men came."

The patterns were all quite similar. As Bragg and Col went forward over the rock face in Nob's direction, they encountered, over and over, the shapes of turtles, birds and sometimes snakes. The "beasts" turned out to be giant platypus. And everywhere, in a context with the animals — or totems — there were etchings of stick men and women — the sexes plainly and even grotesquely limned with oversize phalluses and breasts.

One other feature ran consistently with the rest. There was always a moon — though never full. This moon was always in its quarter phase and it always shone in the sky directly above the figures of the men and women.

"Over here!" Nob cried. "I've found it."

What Nob had found was a curious variation on all the other petroglyphs.

For sure, the snakes and the birds and the turtles and the platypus were all in evidence — just as the moon and two stick figures, male and female were equally in evidence. But here, there was also another figure — of a kind that had not appeared before. It was a human figure — yes — but not at all the same as the others near which it had been carved.

This human figure had long flowing hair — and the way it had been carved, with multiple streaks and lines, the

23

hair appeared to be white and possibly the hair of an albino. One arm was stretched out sideways, one arm was held down flat against the figure's side. One leg was longer than the other — and the shorter leg was resting on a sort of triangular shoe, or little box.

"What does it mean?" Bragg asked — expecting Nob to answer with assurance.

But — "nobody knows," said Nob. "There's been all kinds and every sort of conjecture. Most archaeologists think its a shaman figure — maybe a witch. It's female, at any rate."

Bragg looked down at the magical figure cut at his feet and a curious, worrying noise set up in his mind: a kind of racket, like a buzz-saw carving trees.

Nob said: "this is where she wanted to be scattered. Just here over these figures and in the sky."

He turned away — and so did Col as Bragg undid the hook that held the lid in place. Before he opened the lid, he kissed the box and then he withdrew Minna's ashes handful by handful and threw them like an offering upon the stones.

The plane was now approaching San Francisco and Bragg could see the Janis Joplin girl going into one of the washrooms or — as she would say — the head. The sight of her, so Minna-like, was jarring since he'd just finished scattering Minna's ashes in his mind.

Col said: "twenty minutes and we're there."

Bragg wasn't sure he wanted that.

He could see the great grey fog that lay above the city and he thought of all the men and women living in its shadow. Here was a city, he thought, that once was the symbol of all the bright hope in the Western world. And now it was a city gripped by terror, numbed with the shock of AIDS.

We have probably come to the end, for all we know — Bragg thought — of human congress. Certainly, it marked the end of human passion as it affected homosexuals — and, more and more, it affected everyone.

All his life, he'd been taught that he was an outcast — part of a scourge upon mankind. All the offshoots of this thinking had always seemed, to Bragg, to be so ridiculous and paranoid, he'd never paid attention. Now, there were people down in that city who were dying because of sex.

He tried not to dwell on this and he put it aside.

The Janis Joplin girl came out of the head and she was barely recognizable. Somehow, she had managed a magical transformation and the cotton shirt and the frizzy hair had been replaced with a neat, black dress and a chignon. She was, in fact, quite beautiful and appeared to be serene about the prospect before her. "I'm going home, now, to be married," she had said. "And I'm not allowed to be sad...."

All at once, Bragg went racing back in his mind to the very first day he'd realized he was in love with Minna Joyce. She, too, had worn a neat, black dress and had put her hair up thus. How long ago this was, it hardly mattered. Ten years: twelve. How wonderful she was — had been — would always be, stepping forward into their lives together with so much confidence and joy.

Dear God, he thought. I know now why she wanted her ashes scattered there at Ku-Ring-Gai. It was the joy and the liveliness — the sense of endless celebration that clung to all the figures in the rock. And the figures where the shaman stood — the very place where Minna's ashes fell...

It was not a shaman at all.

He knew it, now, as surely as Minna must have known it the minute she encountered the crazy figure cut in the rock so utterly and absolutely unlike all the others.

It was a child. A child. The child of the two stick figures rejoicing by its side beneath the moon. And the child had long, albino hair and one six-fingered hand stretched out for all the world to see forever — and it stood on one good leg and one short leg, for which her parents had made a loving box. Forever. And forever visible.

A shiver went down his back. And he knew right then, as he waited to debark the plane, that he would return to Ku-Ring-Gai with Stella on his shoulder. Or his hip.

A GIFT OF MERCY

When Minna Joyce first laid eyes on Stuart Bragg, she told herself to remain calm. This was back in 1975 when she was still in her waitress phase and working for a man whose name was Shirley Felton. Shirley ran what Minna called The Moribund Cafe on Queen Street West. It was really called the Morrison Cafe, because it was in the Morrison Hotel — a rummy dive for drunks and crazies, now defunct, on the north-east corner of Shaw and Queen. Minna had been working there since late July of the previous year and the reason she gave for taking such a job was that she had to keep her eye on the Queen Street Mental Health Centre, just across the road.

"You never know, my dear," she had said to one of her park-bench friends, "what they'll do behind your back." Also, there was the vaguest hope that her mother — the newly remarried Mrs Harold Opie — might drift by one day and find her cast-off, screwed-up daughter working behind the counter in The Moribund Cafe — drop dead of shock and thus spare the world the continued menace of her presence. "And that, my dear, would be worth the price of admission!"

As to why Mrs Harold Opie — the ex-Mrs Galway Joyce — might be adrift at all on Queen Street, only Minna Joyce could imagine. Perhaps her cool stability was really less than it seemed and she was looking for yet another masochist crazy enough to marry her. Galway Joyce and Harold Opie had both been mad enough to do so — and, from what Minna knew of her mother's most recent marriage, Mister Opie was already on the way out the door. But whatever the reason might be, Minna Joyce was content to believe in its probability and dream of its eventuality.

Now, in the depths of winter, Stuart Bragg had just walked through the door and Minna — who was leaning down to place a cup of coffee and a plastic spoon beneath the vacant stare of one of the Moribund's regular customers — felt the draught and looked up to see who might have entered.

There he was, and her body held its breath while her mind went racing.

A blizzard was going on outside and Bragg had brought it with him through the door. His hair was white with snow and he wore a long, black coat. The storm raged up against the plate glass window at his back and the way it blew, it looked as if it had pursued him, eager to engulf him.

Bragg had the look of one who bore a message — lost and uncertain as to whom the message must be given.

Me, said Minna's mind. *He's come here looking for me.*

But, of course, he hadn't. He was just another stranger in from Queen Street and Minna was quickly reconciled to believing that was good enough. Strangers were her specialty and those who were pursued by storms and demons made the best strangers of all. She herself had once been pursued by storms and demons, and, even now, she was still in the process of firing at them over her shoulder — her aim perfected after many years of practice. Only three or four remained at her heels, and, of these, the most persistent were her love of dark red wine and her passion for the written word. This latter was a demon flashing sentences before her eyes with incomprehensible speed — and whose sibilant voice was lower than a man's.

Bragg's eyes searched the restaurant for someone he could trust. Minna was used to this look. She saw it every day, when strangers walked in and were confronted by the faces of the regulars — the rummies and the drugged-out kids, the schizoids and the dead-eyed retainers whose job it was to sweep the snow and rake the leaves at the Queen Street Mental Health Centre. Bragg evaded all these people — caught Minna's eye and turned away from her.

Wait, she wanted to say to him. *I can help you.* Minna recognized the look in his eyes of unrequited sanity — the look of someone terrified of the light in a world lit up with stark bare bulbs. He even squinted, placing his hand along his forehead. Minna stepped forward — but Shirley was already marching down behind the counter.

"Yeah?" Shirley said to Bragg — using his dishrag, polishing the soiled Formica countertop, rearranging the packs of

31

chewing gum piled beside the register. "What can I do you for?"

Minna listened, breathless.

Please don't go away, she was thinking. *Don't go away before we've made contact.*

"I need to make a call," said Bragg. "Have you got a telephone?"

"Sure I got a telephone," said Shirley, "but it ain't for public use. You wanta coffee instead?"

"Thank you, no," said Bragg. "I really do need to make a call." He was eyeing the telephone behind the counter just the way a man who is starving eyes the food on someone else's plate.

"Sorry," Shirley told him. "I got a policy here: no calls."

"Where, then? Where can I find a telephone?"

"'Cross the road in the Centre. Maybe there's a pay phone there."

"Thank you," said Bragg. And he turned to go.

No, said Minna. *You mustn't. We haven't met.*

But he was out the door and the storm was about to have its way with him.

Minna closed her eyes. Why were the lost so beautiful? She couldn't let him go.

"Wait!" she heard herself calling.

Shirley turned in her direction. "What the fuck's with you?" he said to her. "Didn't I tell you no one yells in the Morrison Cafe?"

But Minna was already reaching out for the handle of the door and barely heard him.

Out on the street she looked both ways and hurried to the corner.

"Wait!" she shouted. (What if her mother could see her now?)

Everything was white before her and blowing into her eyes. Peering through the snow, she saw the lights were about to change and she ran out, flat against the wind with her apron clinging to her legs like something desperate, begging to be rescued. Suddenly, there she was on the other side of Queen Street, blindly grabbing for the long, black sleeve of the departing stranger.

"Stop!" she yelled at him. "Stop!"

He turned, alarmed and tried to brush her off — but she dug her fingernails into the cloth and pulled up close to his arm.

The man was truly afraid of her; the look on his face was unmistakable and one she had seen a dozen times before. What had he done that she should have followed him — attacked him in such a panic?

"Please," he said, attempting to be civilized. "Don't."

There she was with her hand on his arm — a perfect stranger, standing in a blizzard out on Queen Street, wearing nothing but an apron over a magenta uniform — and *Minna* traced in thread across the pocket at her breast. And her hair was blowing across her face and he thought: *she's mad as a hatter — and beautiful as anyone I've ever seen.*

"All right," he said — giving in because it was so evident she wouldn't let go until she'd had her way. "Tell me what's wrong."

"Your name," she shouted at him — each word blown away in the wind. "Tell me your bloody name."

"What?" he shouted back at her. "What?"

Several people, fully cognizant of where they were and what they might be witnessing out in front of the Queen Street Mental Health Centre, huddled on the corner waiting for a streetcar. The way this man and woman were holding on to one another, they looked as if they were locked in a deadly struggle. But she was only waiting for his answer and he was only trying to prevent her from being swept away in the Queen Street traffic.

"Please," she shouted at him — right into his ear. "I have to know who you are!"

Bragg stepped back and stared at her as best he could through the storm. She was holding back the strands of her flowing hair and it was only then that he saw that she was smiling; laughing at her own audacity.

"Oh," he said. "I see."

Very slowly, he grinned, and three months later they were married.

By the time Minna died, the marriage had lasted just over twelve years. During the final months they had lived apart; Bragg in Toronto, Minna in Australia: *just about as far apart as a person can get, my dear*, she had said. *A gift of mercy for us both.*

Later, she had written in one of her final letters that it was more than likely fate was playing one of its better tricks when it devised this ending: terminating events before the thirteenth anniversary of their meeting on Queen Street. *What do people give each other after thirteen years?* she had written. *A baker's dozen of silver cups; one for each year they've remained on speaking terms? How do they celebrate? A game of Russian roulette? Thirteen guns and only one of them loaded? Yours or mine, Bragg? Yours or mine? We'll never know; for which I'm glad.*

One afternoon, after Bragg and Minna had been married

for seven years and were living on Collier Street, Bragg came home and found a stranger in Minna's bed. This was in February of 1983.

Bragg had just gone into the bathroom where he was soaping his hands when he heard somebody cough. At first, he paid no attention, assuming it was Minna. But when the coughing continued, and began to take on the characteristic sounds of someone who was choking, Bragg shut off the taps.

Instantly, there was silence — broken only by the last of the water curling down the drain. Bragg closed his eyes in order to concentrate. There had been too much of this, recently; too many phantom coughers — too much offstage laughter — too many voices behind his back. At its worst, this paranoia prompted him to wonder if Minna was trying to disrupt his life in order to gain some sort of mastery over him.

Pondering why Minna wanted to harm him always brought him back to his senses. No one had loved him more in all his life. *Still, people do the strangest things for love*, he would think, when he lay awake at four o'clock in the morning. *People have killed and people have died for love, though I'd rather not do either....*

Bragg began to dry his fingers, one by one, with a Laura Ashley towel that Minna had given him for Christmas, a double set to go with the Bembridge paper in the bathroom — burgundy pearl-drop flowers with sprigs of dark blue leaves. Bragg would never have spent the money to buy such expensive towels — but Minna would, and had, and Bragg was secretly glad. He loved all things that had to do with water — bathrooms, bathtubs, basins; taps and showers and toilets. He loved the accoutrement of shaving gear and brushes — glass-stoppered bottles of cologne — soap that smelled of pine and cedar — steamy windows — toothbrush glasses…

Bragg was looking in the mirror the way most people do who don't really want to see themselves — eyes askance, afraid of meeting other eyes. He was just about to duck his head and turn the taps back on to wash away the film of soap in the sink when the second bout of coughing began. Leaving the taps to do their work, Bragg went and stood in the hallway, drying his wrists and listening intently.

This time, the coughing did not abate.

The door to Bragg's own room stood ajar beside him, opposite the bathroom. He could see the comforting shapes of the cats where they lay asleep on his pillows: Morphine and Opium, named for their mother, Poppy, who had died on Queen Street. He could also see his wicker chair with its pile of folded laundry — the shirts and pyjamas he had ironed that morning.

Down at the end of the hall, where Minna's bedroom door was closed against a green satin shoe, the coughing became more violent.

Bragg stepped forward.

The green satin toe obtruded into the hallway, giving the impression someone was lurking there behind the door.

"Hello?" he said.

No one answered.

The coughing stopped.

Bragg screwed up his courage and — watching Minna's door as if he expected it to wield a knife — he approached it, holding his breath, until he was toe to toe with the green satin shoe.

He could see that no one was there — and he gave the door a push with his fingertips.

Lying on Minna's bed, more or less beneath the duvet — one foot and both hands sticking out — there was a tiny figure. It was small enough to be a child.

Bragg could not reconcile the dreadful coughing he had heard with what he saw. Two-Ton Tessie might have coughed like that. But not a child.

The room was lit with curtained light, and since the afternoon was drawing to a close, there was little enough of that to filter through the cotton drapes. The warm intensity of Minna's perfume greeted him briefly — riding past him on the draught from the open door. As soon as he moved into the room, however, he was overcome with the stench of someone exhaling gin and sweating nicotine.

To his left, the shape of Minna's blue Boston rocker stood between him and the windows. The coughing had altogether stopped — and had been replaced with the sound of laboured breathing. Bragg went over and opened the drapes and then — despite the February cold — he also opened the windows.

Turning towards the bed, he was able now to see that the shape he had thought might be that of a child was in fact the angular, sunken figure of someone very small and very old. Matted hair was spread across the pillows. Both hands, fisted, were raised above the figure's head. Halfway down the bed, the extruded foot was clothed in a filthy ankle sock.

Bragg went and stood as close to the bed as he could bear and he looked down into the face of a woman who was old and toothless.

Two small eyes looked up at him: terrified. Instantly, the fists descended and drew the duvet over the face — and a wailing sound began to rise from beneath the feathers.

"Help! Help! Man!" Bragg heard. Then; "Man! Man! Help!"

Bragg turned around and fled — not even stopping to close the door.

Standing outside the bathroom, he prayed the voice would go away before the neighbours called the police.

And indeed, it faded — though it did not stop.

Bragg leaned in against the wall.

"Oh, God," he muttered. "Please, not this again...."

Conjuring up the woman's face — smelling the memory of gin and urine — hearing the woman's muffled voice — Bragg went into the bathroom, where he discovered, to his fury, he had not turned off the taps.

Banging them shut, he remained for a desperate moment, clutching the silver faucets. Then he let go and sighed. He looked up, helpless and resigned, met his own eyes in the mirror and smiled against his will.

"Better find somewhere to hide," he said out loud. "Minna has started another crusade on Queen Street."

They had lived on Queen Street long before then, in rooms above a restaurant. The restaurant was not the Morrison Cafe, but of another kind entirely: run by homosexuals and catering exclusively to gays. The clientele that hung about their doorstep was a trial at times. The very young were very beautiful and Bragg would turn away and walk around the block, attempting to gain control of himself.

For the most part, however, their life above the restaurant was centred on themselves — their love for one another and their work. While Bragg was busy writing in their dreadful little kitchen, Minna spent hours with her notebook, leaning along the window-sill, staring down at all the people walking in the street. Always, these people seemed to be inadequately dressed. Always, there seemed to be an inadequate number of umbrellas; was everyone, as always, mistaking April for spring?

Minna was not a waitress, now. That phase was over and the married phase had begun. Demon Number Two was hard at work in her and she was writing every day in her cloth-bound notebook. Bragg of the blizzard and the long, black coat had turned out to be a budding writer, whose stories had already garnered him a name and a reputation for excellence. They were living on Queen Street not because Bragg had chosen it or even approved of the locale — but only because it seemed to be where Minna Joyce belonged.

Sometimes, early of a morning, the man across the street would come to his window and fling it up — and stand there shaking his fist and shouting obscenities every time a streetcar passed. One day, Minna had brought her note-book and her coffee to the window-sill, when she saw this man take off his clothes and fling them, item by item, onto the top of a streetcar stalled below him. What he wanted, so it seemed, was to get the streetcar's attention — but even now, with it stopped defenceless at his doorstep, the streetcar and its occupants remained oblivious.

Minna had not known what to do about this man. Certainly, she understood his desperation. There was nothing offensive about his nakedness — all its sexuality was masked in rage — and he himself made nothing of it. His clothing had simply become his arsenal — all he had of missiles in the moment. When the streetcar had at last departed, the man had retreated into his darkened room, and in the lulls between the passing traffic, Minna could hear him wailing like a child.

Two days later, Minna had taken up her post, prepared

with pen in hand to continue the saga of the Man Who Hated Streetcars. His story already filled a dozen pages of her notebook.

The sky, that morning, was blue and full of promise. May Day was only a weekend away and the owner of the produce shop across the street had set out buckets of daffodils and tulips, paperwhites and carnations on the sidewalk. Women going to work in the office buildings on Bay Street wore their spring coats and colours. The students making their way towards Bathurst Street and Spadina Avenue wore an array of overalls and sweaters and rode an army of ten-speed bikes. Someone above her was playing a recording very loud of "Goodbye Yellow Brick Road." The sound of Elton John's voice had ridden through the whole of Bragg and Minna's winter, and there it was again, to get them into spring:

> *When are you gonna come down?*
> *When are you going to land?*
> *I should have stayed on the farm,*
> *I should have listened to my old man.*

Minna began to tap out the rhythms with her pen against her coffee mug.

> *You know you can't hold me forever,*
> *I didn't sign up with you.*
> *I'm not a present for your friends to open,*
> *This boy's too young to be singing the blues....*

The man across the street appeared to be singing, too. Except that Minna knew better. The expression on his face was not quite right for singing a song, unless the song was *La Marseillaise*. His mouth was opening far too wide and his eyes were closed too tight. His neck and the muscles in his chest were scarlet and distended: alarming. All the while he sang or shouted, the poor man seemed to be fighting with his window — beating his fists against the latch and heaving his weight against the frame.

Minna stopped singing.

"Bragg?"

She stood up. Bragg didn't answer — locked in the other world beneath his fingers, mouthing the sentences he wrote.

Minna looked back across the road.

Up above, the music kept on spinning like a spider:

> ... goodbye yellow brick road,
> Where the dogs of society howl.
> You can't plant me in your penthouse,
> I'm going back to my plough.

Down in the street, the traffic was piling up and a pair of streetcars had been surrounded by a horde of milk trucks and taxicabs. Nothing was able to move and the worst of it was, the man in the window had begun to panic. Perhaps he imagined the streetcars had come to parlay with him; make their peace and go away forever. But how could they hope to hear him if he couldn't open his window?

Minna could see he had failed altogether to budge the sash. Apparently, this was more than the man could bear, and she watched in horror as he ran away and returned with a baseball bat.

"Bragg?" she whispered. "Hurry...!"

The man began to beat out all his panes of glass, and because the shards were falling to the sidewalk, people started to run for cover. Not an umbrella in sight.

"Stop!" Minna cried.

The man was climbing onto his window-sill.

In Minna's mind was the thought: *if only Bragg would*

come and help me.... But Bragg had reached the climax of his story and was shaping it in perfect cadences, every word and every sentence judged against a count of syllables. He used a thesaurus for this and just at that moment he was looking for a two-beat word for *inhibition*.

Minna and the streetcar man, it seemed, were alone in their private vacuum.

"Stop!" she cried again.

To no avail.

By the time Bragg surfaced and at last appeared, the vacuum had been shattered.

Just as the man had risen onto his toes and leapt, Minna had put her hand through the glass in order to break his fall.

"What in the name of heaven did you think you were trying to do?" Bragg asked her in the Emergency Ward of St. Michael's Hospital. A doctor had wrapped a bandage around the stitches in her wrist — and Minna had been told to lie on her back for half an hour, until the sedation took effect.

"Stop him," she said, "of course."

Then she had looked away at the painted, peeling wall, closing her eyes and praying that Bragg had not been able to read her mind. *Stop him, of course*, is what she had said. But that was not quite true. In the moment, her hope had been that she would catch him; catch the man with her hand held out, the way you catch the rain.

While Minna gave the appearance of having fallen quietly to sleep, Bragg sat down on the iron chair beside the bed and took a slip of paper out of his pocket.

Inhibition, he read.

Stricture.
Hindrance.
Restraint.
None of these was right.

It took him roughly half an hour to decide. The word he chose was *impasse.*

Stuart Bragg's background provided him with money: just enough to buy a house — not enough to avoid a mortgage.

Shortly after the man had leapt to his death on Queen Street, Bragg began to think about a house where Minna would be safe from the influence of visible suicides and where the detritus of humanity wouldn't be on parade for her perusal every time she wandered to the window.

Bragg did not yet understand, back then, that Minna didn't "wander" anywhere. Nothing she did was done by chance and if he had only read her notebooks (not that she wanted him to) he would have discovered she was keeping meticulous track of how the people down on the street were faring. This was her journal of despair — but not her own despair. Somewhere, deep in the body of the note-book, written in a margin, were the words: *and what of me? I cannot articulate and have no desire to tell where I have been and where I am going. Surely this is dangerous. What am I hiding? When will it surface?*

But that was all there was of that. No conjecture. No predictions.

Nonetheless, Bragg had felt the urgency burgeoning in Minna's restlessness and he feared her growing habit of silence. Changing the milieu might not be the whole and only answer — but surely it must be part of it.

He, too, wanted to escape. He wanted trees and grass to

re-enter his life. He wanted — even once a week — to make his way down the stairs and into the street without the ever-present threat of someone else's panic waiting to grab his sleeve. Or kill his cats.

Poppy, his aging Burmese female, had been driven under the traffic by a man with a stick, who was convinced all cats were spreading the devil's message in their scat. Two days later, Bragg announced he'd found a house on Collier Street, south of Rosedale, north of Bloor. It had three trees and a high board fence at the rear — and, across the road, a park.

Minna was urged, by dint of Bragg's enthusiasm, to go at least and take a look. "Give the house a chance to work its magic on you, Min," Bragg said. "It has the feel of a winner."

Minna was guarded about her reaction. The fact was, she liked it well enough — but it had two drawbacks she didn't want to discuss with Bragg. One was its proximity to Rosedale — Rosedale having been the scene of childhood traumas and, therefore, the only place in all of Toronto to which she had sworn she would never return. The other drawback to the house on Collier Street was its abundance of bedrooms: one too many for Minna to tolerate with any ease. She feared — had feared — would fear forever — Bragg's desertion of their mutual bed. But she couldn't say these things, and so it was that she gave her assent to the move and one month later, she and Bragg and the remaining cats moved in. Bragg's being able to afford it made it easier to reconcile. But Minna told herself that was not the end of Queen Street in her life.

Down in the kitchen, Minna was drinking her dark red wine and setting the table. A painted wooden tray, Bragg noted, had been lifted onto the counter and sat there waiting to be set. Somehow, the empty tray was like a threat, because it meant the woman in the bed was going to be fed up there, nurtured and urged to stay.

"What the hell is going on?" he said.

Minna said: "I'm making dinner. Any objection?" She was belligerent and defensive all at once. Bragg could see the bottle of Côtes-du-Rhône, sitting on the counter beside the empty tray, had been half emptied already.

"Yes, I have objections," he said — and got himself a glass. "I have objections to that woman's presence in your bedroom. Who the hell is she?"

Minna put her hand out and lifted the Côtes-du-Rhône out of Bragg's way just as he was about to reach for it. "Why not open a bottle of your own?" she said. "I'm keeping track of how much I drink," she added — and filled her glass.

Bragg went and rummaged in the corner cupboard — where he found a bottle of Beaujolais and two more bottles of Côtes-du-Rhône. Choosing the Beaujolais, he found the corkscrew, still with Minna's cork impaled on it.

Minna, holding her drink and cigarette in one hand, was standing at the stove and stirring something in a pot with the other. Her back was to him. All the while Bragg was opening the Beaujolais, he was watching Minna's back to see what it would tell him.

Nothing.

At last, having filled his glass, he said: "you haven't answered my question, Minna. Who is that woman in your bed?"

"Her name is Elizabeth Doyle," said Minna. "Calls herself Libby."

Bragg found Minna's cigarettes — took one and lighted it. "And?" he said.

45

"And what?"

"Oh, for Christ's sake!" he exploded — spilling his wine. "Who the hell is she? What the fuck is she doing here?"

Minna laid down the wooden spoon and walked across to the painted tray. She began to lay out silver and a napkin on its blue and yellow birds. Her voice was shaking when she answered — but she resisted raising it.

"I found her on Queen Street," she said as evenly as possible. "Standing in the rain."

Bragg gave a sigh and sat at the table.

Minna turned and looked at him.

"It's all right, Bragg," she said. "She's perfectly harmless."

"I'm glad to hear it," said Bragg. "After you've fed her, what then?"

"She'll more than likely go back to sleep," said Minna. "I would, if I was her. I don't think she's had a decent sleep in ninety years." She set a wine glass next to a pepper grinder on the tray and looked around for an extra salt shaker. "My guess is, she's homeless — but she won't admit it."

"Did she admit she was a lush?" Bragg asked.

Minna paused and then went on with her search. "Maybe if I was living on the street I'd be a lush, too," she said.

"You'd be a lot of things, wouldn't you. *If*," said Bragg. He was absolutely furious because he felt the trap of reason closing around him. Surely, all of this would end with Minna saying *only a monster would have left her there...*

"Where will you sleep?" he said.

Minna didn't hesitate a second.

"Why, with you, of course."

Bragg crushed out his cigarette and pinched another one — lighting it at once. He got up, retrieved the bottle of Beaujolais and sat down. He finished the wine already in his glass and filled the glass again.

46

"It doesn't make sense," said Bragg. "Bringing home strangers. It's crazy."

"I brought *you* home from Queen Street," she said.

Bragg did not utter.

Minna filled her glass and then said: "why is it crazy? What would you have done? Leave her there?"

"I wouldn't have been on Queen Street to begin with," said Bragg, "if I were you. I wouldn't even be there if I were me. What the hell were you doing?"

"Research."

This was true. Bragg knew that. Minna's book was going to be all about the denizens of Queen Street.

Then he said something cruel — wishing he wasn't saying it — saying it anyway. "What makes you think you have to do research, Minna? Tell me what it is you don't already know about these people."

Minna turned away — got down three large plates and put them in the oven to warm them.

"Aren't you going to answer me?" said Bragg — pressing his luck.

"Answer you about what?"

"Your goddamned research, Minna. Your goddamned research and your goddamned need to throw yourself under the wheels of that woman upstairs."

"I..."

"What's there to know about these goddamned people you don't already know? They're crazy, Minna. They're *crazy!*" He was almost yelling.

"So — they're crazy," she said. She still didn't want to raise her voice. She only wanted this to end.

"Then why don't you go and live with them — instead of bringing them back here?"

"Why should I do that, Bragg?"

47

"Because you're one of them, that's why. You and the goddamned Morrison Cafe."

Minna subsided. Everything turned to ice inside her.

"Fine," she said. "I'm one of them. That settles it."

Nothing more was said.

Bragg sat out the interim while Minna took Libby Doyle her tray — and he drank another glass of wine.

When Minna came down about five minutes later, she got out another tray and began to set it with silver.

"What are you up to, now?" said Bragg — alarmed.

"Nothing unusual," said Minna. "I just thought I'd take my dinner upstairs. Eat with my own kind. That sort of thing. That's all." She plonked another bottle of Côtes-du-Rhône on the tray.

Bragg said: "I'm not going to let you do this, Minna. That woman is going to leave this house and you are going to return to your senses."

He stood up and almost knocked his wine glass over. Minna watched him carefully. Maybe she was secretly glad he was doing this. She couldn't tell. But she didn't challenge him — and when he made his move to the door, she didn't try to stop him.

Like anyone growing up knowing there was money in the bank, Bragg had never given it a lot of thought. Perhaps if he had been of another generation — the one emerging in the 1980s, for instance — he might have found more delight in money than he did; far more joy in having it — far more anguish when it disappeared. But having come of age in the 1960s, Bragg's relations with money were indifferent: cordial enough if a dividend passed his way, but unconcerned if riches eluded him.

I've never felt I was writing for money, he was to say much later on. He wrote to make his living, he told a journalist, not to make his fortune. His work was well if not highly regarded. Whenever a new Bragg piece appeared, his severest critics — other writers — always said: *the best is yet to come.* He wrote short novels and he wrote long stories — a paradox for which he had no explanation. The first of his stories — still regarded as his best — had already been published before the advent of Minna in his life.

The thing about Bragg that gave his writing its "voice" was his savage sense of humour — laughter that only reached the page; he had no gift for laughter in his life. Bragg himself — though he shunned the practice, even the thought of analysis — was perfectly aware of the written humour's source. All his life he had known he was set aside from the comfortable mass by the fact of his homosexuality.

Some who where close to him — one of his brothers, one of his aunts — had forgiven him. Most of those close to him had not. Bragg well knew he need not be "forgiven"; he knew that "forgiveness" in the given view could only be construed as a kind of arrogance. *What kind of person —* Bragg had allowed a character beneath his hand to ask — *would think it appropriate to confer forgiveness on a chap for being born?* After all, Bragg had a cousin who was retarded and an aunt who was schizophrenic. Had anyone forgiven *them?* If they had, Bragg might have hauled out a gun and shot them for their impertinence. Still, he recognized the impulse in his brother and his aunt to be forgiving. They had been nurtured in the Church, where forgiveness had no connection to understanding. Bragg's other brother and their father had urged him to seek a "cure." His mother, long since dead, had been convinced the sin was in her. His birth had, therefore, been a punishment laid upon her

49

immortal soul. So much, Bragg concluded, for the gentle mercy of God.

So this was his private fund of rage: the rage that produced his written humour — and the rage, by most accounts, that saved his writing from the spoils of too much darkness.

One day, however, Bragg would free the bitch inside him — or the bitch inside him would cut her leash, break loose and savage the neighbours. But he didn't know that yet. He still contained her on the page — where she was always confined to barking through the mouths of those Bragg least resembled in his private being. He did not believe in writing as revenge.

Minna Joyce could not let go of Queen Street West. Or perhaps it was that Queen Street West would not let go of Minna Joyce. She had gone there to take up residence with a sense of mission. When that had been, she could not recall, probably because she had gone there so often in her mind before she had sought out lodgings there and jobs. More than likely the move had taken place in 1971 or '72. This would be after her parents had divorced and Minna was in her early twenties.

The Galway Joyces and their only remaining child had lived in the depths of Rosedale up on Douglas Drive beyond the Glen Road Bridge. They had lived there all of Minna's life and during the time when her sister, Alma, had been carried off by a burst appendix. *Carried off* had been Galway Joyce's phrase. Mrs Joyce — whose first name was Lue Anne — had been more forthright and more unforgiving: the doctors had done it and that was that. They had failed to gauge the progress of Alma's condition and they had *let her die before relief could reach her.* Minna had been nine when Alma died and Alma had been eleven and, again in Lue Anne's words, *the First-Prize Winner of all the children ever born.* In Minna's words, she grew up after Alma's death as "the First-Prize Winner, my dear, of all the unwanted children ever born." But that was fine, in Minna's terms, because it meant she would never have to feel obliged to love her parents.

Queen Street West and, in fact, the whole of Parkdale offered a world of unwanted people — the only people Minna felt any affection for. They lived in the shadow of the Queen Street Mental Health Centre, either having been discharged from its vast and innumerable wards or waiting to enter them. Minna took rooms in several houses — one and then another — moving according to her whims and work. She spent some time as a clerk in a retail outlet, selling bathroom fixtures; then as a dispatcher for a taxi company; then behind the counter in a porno shop, where the magazine covers finally got her down and then, at last, as Shirley Felton's boisterous and rebellious waitress in The Moribund Cafe. And all this while, she was pursued by her storms and demons — red wine and writing consuming all her free time.

Red wine and writing — and people-watching.

The crazies touched and moved her beyond all others: the way they walked, the way they stood, the way they tried to speak. *Just to be seen, Bragg. Just to be seen and heard and acknowledged. That's what they wanted. Witness. Not to be forgotten.*

"Where am I now?" they would say to her. "Can you tell me where I am?"

Minna would listen and she would tell them: "here."

It was the only answer any of them ever understood — and no one else had ever said it to them. *Here is where you are: with me.* Everyone else was always saying to them: "you're on Queen Street."

Over time — in spite of everything, including love of Bragg and love of life — Minna could not abandon the crazies and the winos out on Queen Street. She couldn't stay away from *here.* She tried, but it was a true addiction: something in the nerve ends needing a constant fix. She kept going back for more. This way, she had encountered Libby Doyle, who was now upstairs, about to be evicted from the only bed she had known in over a year.

Soaked with rain and standing in an alley down behind the Marmax Bargain Centre, Libby Doyle had been drinking gin from a bottle concealed in one of her Eaton's shopping bags. She had worn an old dark dress at least four sizes too large and a pair of children's yellow rubber boots. Her hair was only partly covered with a green plastic triangle Minna soon perceived was the scissored corner of a garbage bag and she had been singing songs. "Don't Sit Under The Apple Tree" had been one of them. "Paper Doll" had been another. "I'll Be Around" and "You'll Never Know." War songs from her heyday.

Looking at her, Minna had decided her heyday must have been terrific. What an extraordinary face she had — Elizabeth Doyle, with wide-set eyes and high-pitched bones — a raging beauty, back in 1942. And now what other people would call a hag.

"Can I drink with you?" Minna said.

"You can, indeed," said Libby Doyle and offered her gin at once, the way all rubbies do. "Do you know where we can get another?"

Minna said: "yes, I do" and drank from the bottle — hating gin, but doing it for Libby's sake.

After her third or fourth *pull on the tit* (as Libby Doyle

described it) Minna said: "there's a pub round the corner we can go to." She really wanted just to get Libby in somewhere and out of the rain. But Libby said: "they kick me out of pubs. It's 'cause I always sing."

Minna said: "then I'll take you home."

"I'm home right here," said Libby Doyle. And she indicated the alley filled with large-sized cardboard packing crates from the Marmax Bargain Centre.

"No," said Minna. "I mean, I'll take you home with me."

"Oh," said Libby Doyle. "I suppose you wouldn't have a glass I could drink from, would you?"

"Yes," said Minna. "I have lots of glasses."

"Good," said Libby Doyle. "These goddamned bottles are always breaking my teeth."

Minna laughed and they made their way to the curb with all of Libby's shopping bags and Minna hailed a cab and brought the old woman home to Collier Street.

Nothing was said along the way until they were stopped for a light on Markham Street and Libby, wiping the window clear of steam, peered out and said, with perfect sobriety and without a trace of envy: "my daughter lives in that house there; the one with all the windows."

Minna looked and saw a perfectly restored brick house set back beyond a wooden deck. A cat was staring down from a lighted room on the second floor.

"The cat's name is Rosie," said Libby Doyle. And they drove away.

After an extended silence, Minna heard footsteps on the staircase: Libby's first — Bragg's second. Then she heard Bragg speaking in the hallway.

"Stay there, Mrs Doyle," he said. "If you move an inch, I'll call the police." Then he pushed open the kitchen door and let it swing closed behind him.

Minna blinked.

Bragg's arms were filled with a wild array of plastic carry-all bags and little boxes and bits of clothing. What had he done to Libby Doyle?

"May I just show you," he said, "before I transport your lady friend back to Queen Street, how she has repaid your hospitality?" He said this with an icy coldness and then he began to dismantle the array of goods in his arms – tersely naming every item as he set it down on the kitchen table.

"One pair of satin shoes," he said. "Green. One blue cotton dress. One wool jacket. Three pairs of freshly laundered men's underwear – *mine*," he said. "One knitted jersey – *mine*. *Your* old watch. *Your* photograph of me in its silver frame. One jar of olives – god knows where *that* came from – one bottle of aspirin – and *this*…"

Bragg held out the long silver cord of Minna's French dressing gown.

Minna sat frozen.

Bragg didn't understand. He thought her stillness signified that she had learned her lesson: *crazy bag ladies steal.*

But that was not what had frozen her.

"I'm taking her back," said Bragg. "To the Marmax Bargain Centre where you found her. And, by the way, be grateful she didn't kill us in our sleep." He threw a switchblade knife on the table.

Minna still did not move.

Bragg went back into the hall and Minna listened to him hustling the old woman out through the front door and down the walk to his little car and then she heard the car doors slam – one, two – and the whole world drive away. Or so it seemed.

Minna blinked and poured herself another glass of Côtes-du-Rhône.

She reached out and touched the silver cord and lifted it up and held it against her cheek.

Minna tried to banish the picture the silver cord had conjured when Bragg first threw it down: the image — vivid as the photograph of Bragg in his silver frame — of Libby Doyle hanging by her neck in the Marmax Bargain Centre's alley — free at last of her storms and demons.

"I almost saved her," she said out loud. "He simply doesn't understand." She thought of Shirley Felton and his goddamned telephone down at The Moribund Cafe — and the day Bragg had entered her life. "I got a policy," Shirley had said to him. "No calls."

Now, Stuart Bragg had become like that: *no one is allowed to call for help.*

Back in 1964, when Minna Joyce was in her seventeenth year, Lue Anne, her mother, had had her committed — briefly — because she had broken all her family's traditions of silence, propriety and submission. Yelling fits had overcome the child in the worst of places: streetcars and schoolrooms — Britnell's Book Store — Eaton's and Simpsons — church. It had been a nightmare time for everyone concerned, though no one — least of all Lue Anne Joyce — had seemed to understand it was a nightmare most of all for Minna. Minna knew that in the depths of her mother's being she was offering up the child she did not want to the same profession that had killed the child she loved. Minna's committal was nothing less, she surmised, than revenge.

Emerging sedated and sedate at seventeen, Minna had launched herself upon the adult world in a ship as sleek

55

and silent as a deadly submarine. Until her parents were separated and she was able, at last, to leave their Rosedale house and take up life elsewhere — Minna had remained in view upon the surface. But once the divorce was final and all the silverware and Spode and all the securities had been divided, Minna had submerged and gone to live in a rooming-house on Foxley Street in Parkdale. This, for Minna, was a perfect haven — centred in the dark of Crazyland.

Foxley Street ran between Dovercourt and Ossington, both of which provided escape routes via public transport out of the danger zone. Walking every evening in the twilight, wearing her duffel coat and tam, Minna strolled at ease beneath the trees, that spring, across the wide and burgeoning lawns of the Queen Street Mental Health Centre. Whenever she spoke, she spoke to squirrels. If she sang, it was always under her breath. She never yelled, she never cursed and she never once flung herself beneath the heels of authority. Quietly, with dignity and calm, she lay beneath the surface of her tranquillizers, plotting the overthrow of all the conniving mothers in the world — and all the sentimental, ineffectual fathers — not to mention all the obedient, deadly doctors.

It was also then that Minna Joyce began to plot the overthrow of silence.

When Bragg returned that night — he was not alone. Something in that day's events had impelled him to do a thing he had never done before in all the years of his marriage to Minna Joyce.

After leaving Libby Doyle on the pavement, roughly speaking just about where the Man Who Hated Streetcars had died — he drove back to Yonge Street and up to Dundas, where he parked his car in a parking lot and went inside a bar he had heard of long ago. It was called The Cockatoo.

Round about two o'clock that morning, Bragg arrived at Collier Street with a lad called Donald Murray, whom he led inside the house and up the stairs and into his bed.

Minna's door was open and about an hour later — far down the tunnel of the hallway — she saw the shape of Donald Murray as he passed into the bathroom.

There, she thought. *It's done. We've come full circle from the day we met and now our lives will never be the same.*

She was thinking of what Bragg had told her about that call he had wanted to place from The Moribund Cafe.

"I was going to phone a man I'd met and make him a gift of my virginity."

So much for Shirley Felton's policy.

When she slept that night, in all her dreams Minna was yelling *STOP! STOP! STOP!* at the top of her voice on Queen Street in the snow.

FOXES

The face is only the thing to write.

Roland Barthes

All the appropriate people had been forewarned: Morris Glendenning would be coming to the Royal Ontario Museum to do some private research in the Far Eastern Department. He was not to be approached; he was not to be disturbed.

Glendenning's reclusiveness was legendary, made doubly curious by the fact he was the world's best-known communications expert — a man whose public stances and pronouncements had put him at centre stage as long ago as 1965. The thing was, Morris Glendenning could not bear to be seen.

But, as with most eccentric beings, part of what was

eccentric in him seemed determined to thwart whatever else was eccentric. In Morris Glendenning's case, his passion for privacy was undone by his need for warmth — which led to a passion for things made of wool and, as well, to what some considered to be the most eccentric habit of dress in the whole community of North American intellectuals.

He wore old-fashioned galoshes — the kind made of sailcloth and rubber, sporting metal fasteners shaped like little ladders lying on their sides. He was also given to wearing a multiplicity of woollen garments layered across his chest: scarves, sweaters, undervests — each of a pre-scribed colour. He wore, as well, a navy blue beret, pulled down over the tops of his prominent ears. He was six feet, six inches tall and was made, it seemed, almost entirely of bone. His skin was pale, translucent and shining — as if he polished it at night with a chamois cloth. Glendenning's overcoat was blue and had a military cut — naval, perhaps. It was pinched at the waist and almost reached his ankles. In magazine photographs — taken always on the run — Morris Glendenning had the look of Greta Garbo, heading for doorways and ducking into elevators: "*COMMUNICA-TIONS EXPERT ESCAPES YET AGAIN!*"

Mrs Elston, in charge of secretarial work for the Far Eastern Department at the Royal Ontario Museum, had been told by her boss that Glendenning would be turning up on the Friday morning, last week in February. She was quite looking forward to meeting the famous man. Dr Dime, the curator, had instructed her to offer all available assistance without stint and without question. On no account, she was told, was he to be approached by staff. "Whatever help he requires, he will solicit: probably by note...." By mid-afternoon, however, on the day of the visit, Mrs Elston said:

"it doesn't take much to guarantee the privacy of someone who doesn't even bother to show up."

At which point Myrna Stovich, her assistant, said: "but he *is* here, Mrs Elston. Or — *some*one is. His overcoat and galoshes are sitting right there…." And she pointed out a huddled, navy blue shape on a chair and a pair of sailcloth overshoes squatting in a large brown puddle.

"For heaven's sake," said Mrs Elston. "How can that have happened when I've been sitting here all day?"

"You haven't been sitting here all day," said Myrna Stovich. "You took a coffee break and you went to lunch."

The night before, and all that morning, it had snowed. The clouds were a shade of charcoal flannel peculiar to clouds that lower above Toronto at the dirty end of winter. Merely looking at them made you cough. Morris Glendenning had supplemented his already over-protective array of woollen garments with one more scarf, which he pulled down crossways over his radiator ribs and tied against the small of his back. Even before he departed his Rosedale home, he pulled his beret over his ears and bowed his head beneath the elements.

Walking across the Sherbourne Street bridge, Morris set his mind on his destination and, thereby, shut out the presence of his fellow pedestrians. His destination at large was the Royal Ontario Museum but his absolute destination was its collection of Japanese theatre masks.

Long after midnight, Morris Glendenning had sat up watching the snow eradicate the garden and the trees

63

beyond his windows. Now, he was tired. And reflective. Progress with his current work had stalled, partly due to the residue of sorrow over his wife's midsummer death and partly due to the fact he had published a book two months later, in September. The work itself — the massing of materials, the culling of ideas — had been passing through an arid stage and it was only in the last few days that he'd begun to feel remotely creative again. Not that he hadn't traversed this particular desert before. Far from it. After every piece of exploration — after every publication of his findings — after every attempt at articulating the theories rising from his findings, Morris Glendenning — not unlike every other kind of writer — found himself, as if by some sinister miracle of transportation, not at the edge but at the very centre of a wasteland from which he could extract not a single living thought. For days — sometimes for weeks — his mind had all the symptoms of dehydration and starvation: desiccated and paralyzed almost to the point of catatonia. Five days ago it had been in that state. But, now, it was reviving — feeding again, but gently. And all because of a chance encounter with a photograph.

The photograph had appeared in a magazine called *Rotunda,* published by the Royal Ontario Museum; and it showed a Japanese theatre mask recently purchased and brought from the Orient. "Fox," the caption read. But it wasn't quite a fox. It was a *human fox,* alarming in its subtle implications. Reading about it, Morris Glendenning discovered it was one of three or four others — a series of masks created for a seventeenth-century Japanese drama in which a fox becomes a man. Each of the masks, so the article informed him, displayed a separate stage in the transformation of a quintessential fox into a quintessential human being. Glendenning's curiosity was piqued — and more than piqued; a trigger was pulled in the deeps of his consciousness. Something had been recognized, he realized, and he felt the reverberations rising like bubbles to the surface: signals, perhaps — or warnings.

He very well remembered reading David Garnett's horror story *Lady Into Fox* — that masterful, witty morality tale in which the English "hunting class" is put in its place when one of its wives becomes a fox. But here, in these Japanese masks, the process had been reversed. It was the fox who took on human form. On the other hand, this was more or less standard procedure when it came to balancing the myths and customs of the Orient against the myths and customs of the West. Almost inevitably, the icons and symbols employed by custom and by myth were opposites: white in the Orient, black in the West for mourning; respect for, not the arrogation of nature; death, not birth as access to immortality.

Whose fate, Glendenning had written in the margin next to the provocative photograph, *is being fulfilled within this mask? The fox's? Or the man's?*

Clipping the whole page out of the magazine, he slipped it into a file marked *Personae,* and five minutes later, he retrieved it — held it up in the snow-white light from the windows and stared at it, mesmerized. The question became an obsession. Looking into the lacquered face of the mask he imagined stripping off the layers of the human face. Not to the bone, but to the being.

The blooming of this image took its time. It occurred to him slowly that under the weight of all his personal masks, there was a being he had never seen. Not a creature hidden by design — but something buried alive that wanted to live and that had a right to life.

"Foxes into humans," he said out loud as he watched the photograph. *Their choice, not ours.*

Standing in the bathroom, later that afternoon, something sent a shudder through his shoulders and down his back when, in the very instant of switching on the light, he caught the image of his unmasked self in the mirror. And he noted, in that prodding, ever-observant part of his brain — where even the death of his wife had been observed with the keenest objectivity — that what had been unmasked had not been human. What he had seen — and all he had seen — was a pair of pale gold eyes that stared from a surround of darkness he could not identify.

Half an hour later, Morris picked up the telephone and placed a call to the Curator of the Far Eastern Collection at the Royal Ontario Museum, who happened to be his old acquaintance, Harry Dime. What privileges could Harry Dime afford him? Could he inspect the Japanese masks alone?

Privately, Harry Dime would later conclude he should have said no. For all his own awareness of intellectual curiosity, he had no sense at all of the dangerous threshold at which Glendenning stood. Dime had forgotten that, when he returned with these treasures from another time, he brought them with all their magic intact. Not with ancient spells, of course, since all such things are nonsense

— but the magic they released in others: in those who beheld them without the impediment of superstition.

On the snowy Friday morning, Morris Glendenning debated whether to walk or to chance the subway. Chancing the subway might mean recognition, and given the loss of time that recognition inevitably produced, he decided to walk. Walking, he was certain no one would see him — let alone recognize him. *How many eyes,* he once had said to Nora, his wife, *meet yours on a crowded avenue?*

Bloor Street on a Friday is always massed with shoppers, most of whom, Glendenning noted, like to give the appearance of worldly indifference. *I could go in and buy that coat if I wanted to,* they seemed to be telling themselves. *But I won't do that today, I'll do that on Monday. Maybe Tuesday...* Their impassivity was almost eerie and it troubled Morris Glendenning.

The street, for all its people and all its motor traffic, was silent beneath the falling snow. Morris could see his own and everyone else's breath. If he paused, he could count the breaths and he could take the pulse of where he stood — each breath embracing so many heart beats — all the heart beats racing, lagging — all the secret rhythms of all the people visible in the frosted air. Even the motor traffic gave the appearance of being alive; as much an appearance of life as the people gave with their wisps and plumes of vapours. In behind the windows of these vehicles, the faces peering out of the silence were reflected in the clouds of glass that fronted Harry Rosen's; Cartier's; Bemelmans; Eddie Bauer's. Holt Renfrew...moon phases; passing on Bloor Street.

Morris Glendenning could feel the subway tumbling beneath him, not like an earthquake — merely an indication that something was there, alive and at work, whose underground voice made no more sound than voices make in dreams. Morris paused at the corner of Bellair Street and watched a man he had intimately known in boyhood wander past him with his eyes averted. Later on, both of them would say: *I saw old so-and-so out on Bloor Street, today. He looked appalling; dead...*

I saw old so-and-so today. We passed.

Here, Morris thought, was a kind of debilitating apartness — an apartness that once had been entirely foreign to all these people: the ones who were perfect strangers and the ones who were intimate friends.

We needed each other. That was why we looked each other in the eye. We needed each other. Morris clenched his jaw, afraid that perhaps his lips had been moving over the words. *We've always shared this dreadful place — these awful storms — this appalling climate — and we knew we couldn't afford to be alone. But now...*

Now he was approaching the final stretch of Bloor Street before the stop at Avenue Road, where he would wait for the light to change, the way he had waited there for over forty years.

Beyond the veils of snow he could see the vaguest hint of neon, red in the air above him: *Park Plaza Hotel* — though all he could see was part of the *z* and part of the final *a*.

A small crowd of people formed near the curb and Morris Glendenning was aware, all at once, how many of them wore fur hats. A dozen fur hats and fifteen heads.

Not one person was looking at any other; only Morris Glendenning, counting. Why were they so unconcerned with one another? When had they all become collectively impassive?

Probably last Tuesday.

Morris smiled. Rhetorical questions formed the backbone of his profession, but he delighted in providing stupid, banal and irritating answers. It was a form of private entertainment.

Still, it affected everything they did — this intractable indifference. It affected the way they walked, he observed — the speed with which they walked — their gait, as they made their way along the street. They moved, Morris thought — gazing at them through the falling snow — with the kind of apathy acquired by those whom something — bitterness? — has taught that nothing waits for those who hurry home. It came to him slowly, standing on the curb at Avenue Road and Bloor, that, when he rode on the subway and was recognized, it was not their recognition of him that mattered: but their hope that he — in all his ballyhooed wisdom and fame — might recognize them and tell them who they were. *I know you from somewhere:* that's what they yearned for him to say. *I know — I recognize who you are.*

In the cellars at the ROM, there is a labyrinth of halls and passageways that leads, through various degrees of light and temperature, to various sequestered rooms where various treasures lie in wait for someone to come and give them back their meaning. Bits and pieces, shards and corners of time — numbered, catalogued, guessed at.

Morris Glendenning stood in one of these rooms — perspiring, it so happened — holding in his fingers, his fingers encased in white cotton gloves — the very mask he had encountered first in its photographed image.

The door behind him was closed.

The room — effectively — was sound-proofed by its very depth in the cellars and its distance from the active centre of the building. A dread, white light was all he had to see by: "daylight" shining from computered bulbs.

The mask's companions — three in number — were set out, sterile on a sterile tray: the fox on its way to becoming a man.

He thought of surgery.

He thought of layers.

How small, he thought; *the face is.*

Looking down at the others, beyond the mask he held, he counted over the variations and degrees of change — the fox in his hands at one extreme and the trio of variations, lying on their tray, burgeoning feature by feature into a close proximity of Oriental human beauty. The widely tilted, oval eyes of the fox became the evenly centered, almond eyes of a man. Of *a priest*, so the collection's catalogue had told him.

A priest. So apt a designation, it could only be amusing. Though amusing, of course, in a sinister way.

Morris felt like a marauding and possibly destructive child bent on mischief. A vandal, perhaps. Most certainly, he knew he was trespassing here, the victim of an irresistible impulse: *put it on....*

He had spent over three hours standing there, touching — lifting — contemplating the masks. Around him, resting on shelves and laid out, numbered in other sterile trays was the department's whole collection of Japanese theatre masks. Each mask was hidden: slung in a silk and sometimes quite elaborate bag, the drawstrings tied in neat, fastidious bows.

70

Heads, he thought. *The victims of some revolution.*

The truth was — he dared not open the bags to look.

Some of the bags were darkly stained. And, even though he fully recognized the stains were merely of time and of mildew, he could not bring himself to touch them.

Put it on. Don't be afraid.

Go on.

He held the mask up gently before his face.

He could smell its...what? Its mustiness?

Or was it muskiness?

He closed his eyes and fitted the moulded inner surface over the contours of his bones.

He waited fully fifteen seconds before he dared to open his eyes.

The masks below him, sitting on their tray, were smiling.

Had they smiled before?

He waited, knowing he must not give up until the whole sensation of the mask had been experienced — no matter how long it took.

He thought he heard a noise somewhere out in the corridor. The voice of someone calling.

He held his breath, in order to hear.

Nothing.

And then, as he began to breathe again, he felt the vibrations of a sound between his face and the mask.

Another voice. But whose?

He was a long way off inside himself and standing in another light. A pattern of leaves threw shadows over what he saw perhaps the verge of a clearing somewhere.

Creatures — not human — moved before him.

Foxes.

How elegant they were. How delicate: precise and knowing. Why was he so unconcerned and unafraid?

He began to receive the scent of earth as he had never smelled the earth before: a safe, green, sun-warmed scent.

He looked at his hands. He held them out as far as he could. Human hands — in white gloves. Whose were they?

He tried to speak, but could not.

What emerged, instead of speech, was an inarticulate and strangled sound he had never heard before.

Down below him, where the earth replaced the floor, one of the foxes came and sat at his feet and stared up into his face. It seemed, almost, to know who he was.

Never in all of Morris's life had he been so close to anything wild. He was mesmerized.

Other foxes came, as if to greet him, and they leaned so close against his legs that he could feel their bones against his shins.

The fox that had been the first to come and sit before him narrowed its gaze. It stared so intently, Morris felt that something must be going to happen.

Say something to us, the fox appeared to be saying. Tell us something. Speak to us....

Yes — but how?

Morris was bereft of words. But the impulse to speak was overwhelming. He could feel the sound of something rising through his bowels — and the force of the sound was so alarming that Morris pulled the mask away from his face and thrust it from him — down into the tray from which he had lifted it. When?

How much time had passed. An hour? A day? How far away had he been? Who was he, now? Or what?

He looked — afraid — at the backs of his hands, but they were covered still with the gloves.

The creatures in the tray appeared to stir.

Morris closed his eyes against the notion he was not alone. He did not want to see the floor — for fear the floor was still the sun-warmed ground it had been a moment before.

And yet...

He wanted them back. Their breath and their eyes already haunted him. He waited for their voices — but no voices came.

Morris removed the white cotton gloves. He took a long, deep breath and let it very slowly out between his teeth.

His fingers dipped towards the tray and even before they reached the mask, he smiled — because he could feel the head rising up as sure and real as the sun itself. And when the mask he had chosen was in place, he paused only for seconds before he dared to breathe again, one deep breath, and he found his voice — which was not his human voice but another voice from another time.

Now — at last — he was not alone.

Just before five that afternoon, Mrs Elston was putting the cover on her IBM Selectric and preparing to leave, when she became aware all at once of someone standing behind her.

"Oh," she said — recovering as best she could. "We thought you were not here, Professor Glendenning."

She smiled — but he did not reply.

His enormous height was bending to the task of pulling on his galoshes.

"Shall we be seeing you tomorrow?" Mrs Elston asked.

With his back to her, he shook his head.

"Monday, perhaps?"

But he was buckling his galoshes; silent.

He drew his many scarves about him, buttoned his great-coat, took up his leather bag and started away.

"Professor Glendenning…It was such a great pleasure…"

But Mrs Elston could not reach him. He was gone and the door swung to and fro.

Mrs Elston sniffed the air.

"Myrna?" she said. "Do you smell something?"

Myrna Stovich needed no prompting.

"Sure," she said. "Dog."

"But there *can't* be a dog!" said Mrs Elston.

"Yeah, well," said Myrna. "We also thought there wasn't no Professor Glendenning, didn't we."

"True," Mrs Elston laughed. "You're quite right, my dear. But…goodness! What a day!" she said. "And now we have to go out into all that snow."

"Yeah," said Myrna Stovich. "Sure. But I like the snow."

"Yes," said Mrs Elston, and she sighed. 'I like it, too, I guess." And then she gave a smile. "I suppose I have to, don't I – seeing it's what we've got."

THE SKY

All this began — as most unpleasant things do — on a Monday morning.

Morrison had joined the others out in the open under the sky on the platform of the Rosedale subway station. This was his favourite moment of the day: the last whole view he had of trees and clouds before he was plunged, along with everyone else, into the city's underground depths and the shadows of its looming towers. How fortunate — how right it was — that those who had created the Rosedale subway station had set its platforms squarely beneath the open sky.

Morrison was just in the act of folding his *Globe and Mail* beneath his arm when something fell at his feet that hadn't fallen from his pocket. Looking down, he saw what he took to be a piece of glass — not the cleanest piece of glass in the world, but a rather murky looking piece of glass — and old.

Thinking it was best not to leave such things about for dogs to sit on and children to pick up, Morrison gave the thing a shove with his toe, nudging it towards the edge of the platform. In his mind's eye, he already saw it lying safely amongst the cinders where the only person it could possibly harm would be some man in workman's boots, a peaked cap and one of those orange fluorescent aprons that gave him the authority to be down there between the rails.

Before what Morrison had foreseen could unfold, however, he noted the piece of glass was melting and was not a piece of glass at all. It was a piece of ice. Morrison smiled as he took this in. *I'm just a fool*, he thought. Then he remembered it was May 15th and the sky — so clearly visible — was warm and blue and its only clouds were pale as bits of cotton wool.

Not that dirty pieces of ice the size and shape of cigarette lighters ought to be falling out of the sky at all. But if they were going to fall, they ought to fall in winter.

Except: there it was, you see. Not an icicle; an independent piece of ice. In May.

It had fallen straight down onto the platform right at his feet. He could not pretend it wasn't there. He could not pretend his toe had not been sullied by it. Perhaps if he had pointed it out to someone else... A person should always have a witness. But the thing had melted and a small grey pool of acid-coloured water, dripping onto the cinders, was all the evidence he had.

What if Morrison had imagined it all? Who would be his witness now?

He stood back under the narrow overhang, opened his *Globe and Mail* to the editorial page and tried to concentrate on an irate letter in response to last week's editorial justifying the high cost of living in Markham, Ontario. The train, it seemed, was late; the better to test his patience. He tried to forget the sky and what had fallen. His wife had always wanted them to go and live in Markham, but Morrison had always said they could not afford the luxury of living exclusively with millionaires. Here, in this letter, he had found an ally. Down at his feet, he had found an enemy.

Morrison's wife was having an affair. At first, he had not been certain who the recipient of her illicit affections was — though, over time, he narrowed the field to three. Two of these were business associates and the third was his older brother, David. The fact that David might be courting his wife did not surprise him. It merely alarmed him. Lying along the edge of any sexual relationship between consenting in-laws, there was something illicit Morrison had spied — the pale and sickly fingerprint of incest.

Finally, Morrison concluded David was indeed the culprit but — oh, he thought, *what difference does it make? There's nothing I can do about what is. And trying to interfere will only make them more determined....*

Morrison's lack of surprise and outrage had its foundation in a long and painful awareness of his brother's utter lack of ethics. Their parents had divorced so long ago that Morrison could not recall or name the year. He had gone to live with his mother; David had gone to live with their father. And their father's house was besieged by women. Morrison senior had been a prince of finance and a child of Adonis. The siege of women won the day — and the house, its doors all standing open, fell and was occupied by a long succession of temporary brides, some of whom, as David grew to manhood, strayed in his direction.

David Morrison had made a point, in all his consequent intrigues, of seeking involvement only with the wives of friends. And now his brother's wife, Cynthia. Morrison's theory about this bedding procedure was that Brother David was a lazy man who preferred the easy pickings of his immediate circle to the stress and effort of the open market-place. This was the consequence, surely, of having played in his father's harem. Out in the open market, the women were unknown quantities whose foibles, habits and weaknesses David would have to explore at the expense of his own time and money, whereas the foibles, habits and peccadilloes of the wives of friends, associates (and fathers) came to him free of charge. They fell into his lap like gifts as he lunched and worked and drank with their husbands. The simple questions: *How is Sally? How is Jane?* could produce such lucrative answers as: *a little bored these days, I'm afraid, and wondering what to do with her time....* David would know what to do with her time. Bored wives were best; women on the verge of separation were next to best, but women on the verge of divorce were traps to be avoided at all costs. Next thing a person knew, such women expected you to marry them. This was not what David had in mind at all.

Now that David had focused on Cynthia, Morrison found himself perversely accommodating. He would announce all his business trips in David's presence, letting his brother know that he would *be away in Montreal for two days next week — Wednesday and Thursday*. Also, he would pointedly leave the room whenever Cynthia was on the telephone. Even if she was only talking to her sister — Morrison, believing it was David on the line, would stand up and walk ostentatiously away. Not so he wouldn't hear, but only so David and Cynthia could enjoy their privacy.

Perhaps this apparent lack of gumption on Morrison's part was the legacy of having fallen into his mother's purview after his parents' divorce. Whereas David had enjoyed the playing fields of their father's Forest Hill Playboy Mansion, Morrison had been ensconced as the wailing wall of their mother's Riverdale Leper Colony. She must have spent an hour a day, at least, with her forehead resting on his shoulder — finishing box after box of Kleenex like a tissueholic. She wept as easily as other people speak their names — and as often as the rest of us say *I*. She was devoted to her tears, and the reason lay in her equal devotion to all lost causes. Mrs Morrison, senior, laid out her marriage like a corpse and the wake went on until the day she died. Only then was Morrison freed from the domination of defeat — but, clearly, his freedom came too late. *Qué será, será* became his unproclaimed motto and, under its aegis, he was satisfied to stand aside as David made his move on Cynthia.

The affair had become an open secret — and everywhere that Morrison went, even onto the platform of the Rosedale subway station, he was certain people were watching him — perfect strangers turning to other perfect strangers and saying *there's that fellow Morrison — the one whose wife is sleeping with his brother. The Globe and Mail* — held face-high — provided the perfect hiding place. Except for things that fell from the sky.

Morrison and Cynthia had met over music. The fact is, they had met be<u>cause</u> of music — but Cynthia's way of saying things was smudged with the vernacular of her youth. *We met over music* was always said as if she was chewing gum between each word. She was also prone to saying she was *into Beethoven* — a phrase that bothered Morrison a lot, especially when Cynthia said it at dinner parties. People might accept a certain amount of slang at lunch and cocktail parties, but dinner parties should not be soiled with it. That was Morrison's view, at any rate.

And so, they met because of music. Morrison was devoted to the Toronto Symphony Orchestra and for many years he had been in love, from afar, with one of the violinists. This woman — who played her instrument like an angel — always wore a black velvet dress and she had red hair. Morrison had loved her for over twenty years. Then one Thursday night in the lobby of Roy Thomson Hall, the violinist shed two decades and stood before him on the staircase in the person of Cynthia Box.

Cynthia Box wore a black velvet dress and was with her father. Her hair was a beacon of red — and Morrison's eye was drawn to it at once. Later, in the intermission, Morrison managed to stand beside this woman who hadn't any notion, aside from her radiant beauty, why she might have been chosen for his attentions. Morrison brushed her plump white arm with his fingertips and she was his. No one had ever touched her as if she was a violin before – and her nerve ends tingled until she almost broke into song.

Morrison courted Cynthia Box for the rest of the concert season, plying her with heavy doses of Mahler, Stravinsky and Brahms, and when the season ended with a gala performance of Beethoven's Choral Symphony, Morrison proposed and Cynthia accepted. The wedding was set for the following September, so that by the time of the orchestra's opening concert, their honeymoon would be over and they could attend. One of Morrison's gifts to Cynthia had been a lifetime subscription for two and their Thursday night seats were centre aisle, right next to the rail of the first balcony.

Here it was spring again – May – and, only ten years later, Cynthia was having an affair with David. Morrison could not imagine how he had failed her. Two delightful red-haired children had graced their marriage and one of them – Seiji – was studying the violin. The other – Alexis – was struggling with the cello – though, at the age of eight, she found it rather overpowered her. She was always losing control of its balance in the living-room at home and already it had smashed two Chinese lamps and cracked a number of ashtrays.

Alexis always broke into tears whenever the cello fell, and it seemed too harsh for words to yell at her *tilt it the other way!* or *rest it against your thigh – will you never learn, Alexis!* Morrison – only once – had made the mistake of shouting *give yourself more space, for heaven's sake!* which had brought about the demise of the second Chinese lamp. Nowadays, Alexis practised in the cellar in what her mother referred to as the rec-room – quite unaware that, in leaving her little notes of encouragement for Alexis, *wreck-room* — was not the proper spelling.

By the time the subway train had reached the stop at Queen Street that morning, Morrison had completely forgotten the piece of ice that had fallen at his feet. Heading for Bay Street, he had tucked *The Globe and Mail* under his arm and was thinking about the possibilities of trading in the BMW and going for broke with a Jaguar. Three of the stocks in his portfolio had soared the day before and he thought that for once, instead of consolidating matters — selling short and putting the money in the bank — he might enjoy some of the "excesses" (that was his word) that others around him had indulged in for the last five years. He might even keep the BMW and give it to Cynthia. *There, that's yours*, he would say to her, throwing her the keys. *Use it for running errands, shopping, assignations. Just don't leave it parked in front of David's house — that's all I ask....*

It was a pretty conceit, this imagined speech, like the afternoon light in which he intended to deliver it. He would take her into the living-room — safe, now, from falling cellos — and he would pour them each a drink before he lit the surviving lamps and they would stand together gazing out the windows at the bright forsythia and all the Japanese cherry trees and magnolia trees in bloom along the street — and he would throw her the keys and point at the BMW parked in the driveway. *There, that's yours*, he would say. Et cetera. And then he would gesture beyond the lawn and beyond the sidewalk to where a bronze-blue Jag sat waiting for him. Cynthia would have said *but what will you drive, darling?* And Morrison – casual as Cool Whip, would just say: *that.*

Cynthia, he knew, would secretly be fighting her natural inclination to shout – all her inner voices screaming *the son of a bitch thinks I'm gonna thank him for a goddamned, lousy BMW while he drives around in a Jaguar!*

Then she would thank him and pretend bronze-blue was not her favourite colour. Which, of course, it was.

Morrison worked in the Canada Permanent Building right on the corner of Adelaide and Bay. He was looking at it now – enjoying the richness of its big brass doors and all the brass trim around its arches. He was also enjoying the prospect of reaching his desk and of phoning his broker and asking him to sell the shares that had done so well – and he was waiting right at the curb for the light to change when, all at once, a pigeon fell at his feet.

Morrison looked down and saw that the bird was dead and then, embarrassed, he looked around to see if anyone else had noticed.

Apparently, no one had. Or at least, nobody mentioned it. Morrison appeared to be quite alone with the bird and he considered what he should do.

By now, the light had changed, but Morrison didn't move. The pedestrian traffic flowed around him just as if he was a tree they were used to dealing with every morning. Some went one way – some went the other. It really didn't seem to matter which side they passed on. There he was – and they coped.

Morrison had never encountered a situation like this before. Not in all his years of working in downtown Toronto had he ever seen a dead pigeon. In fact, he had never seen a dead pigeon anywhere. Didn't they fly away to die? Or collapse on rooftops where no one could see them? Weren't they eaten by predators long before they were old?

Well — no. Apparently.

Here it was: a grey and white pigeon — perfectly healthy, by all appearances, not a mark anywhere — dead at his feet.

He wondered whether to step over it or around it. Around it, surely, would be more fitting. Respectful. But — should he really leave it there? What if someone failed to see it and stepped right on it, squishing its ribs and forcing its stomach out through its beak all over their shoes....

If only the pigeon would melt, the way the sky bolt had.

Morrison had reached his desk and was sitting there waiting to phone his broker before it occurred to him what his mind had said. He was hoping Ms Almeda would hurry up with the coffee and the Danish, when it broke through into speech.

"Sky bolt," he said. Out loud.

"The same to you," said Ms Almeda, just then coming through the door with his Boynton mug and his Danish-in-a-napkin. Her suit had liquid sugar stains on it.

"I won't be needing you for half an hour, Ms Almeda," Morrison said. "And when you leave, please close the door."

Ms Almeda smiled her knowing smile and waggled her fingers. "Not you, too, Mister Morrison. Shame on you."

"I beg your pardon?"

"Not you, too," she repeated. "Mister Grainger — you know — he makes these phone calls first thing every morning?"

"No," said Morrison. "I don't know what you mean."

Ms Almeda coloured. Orange beneath her Cover Girl. She stammered. "Oh," she said, "I was really only joking. I shouldn't have mentioned it."

"*Mention it*," said Morrison — narrowing his eyes. Did she mean, by any chance, that Teddy Grainger was placing phone calls to Cynthia?

Ms Almeda had closed herself in a trap — and all she had meant to do was lighten Mister Morrison's day.

"Look, Mister Morrison," she said, "there's a sugar stain from that damned machine all down my front — and I have to dab it in cold water...."

"Tell me about Mister Grainger's calls, Ms Almeda," said Morrison. Then he said: "please."

Ms Almeda held the doorknob very tight in her fist and took a breath and forced her gaze away from Morrison.

"He phones those fantasy numbers," she said. "He closes his door and looks out the window and calls these... numbers."

"Fantasy numbers? You mean he makes them up, Ms Almeda?"

"No, sir. He finds them in the papers. You know..."

"No, I do not know."

"He phones up these numbers and someone talks to him...." She paused — and then she looked him in the eye and said: "sex talk."

Morrison's mouth fell open. All he could think was *Cynthia*. Hadn't Teddy Grainger been in love with Cynthia just around Christmastime. Now, they were talking on the telephone. *Sex talk.*

"May I go?" said Ms Almeda.

Morrison nodded, dazed.

"Shall I close the door?"

"No," said Morrison. "No. Leave it open, for heaven's sake."

Ms Almeda was stepping away from him.

"Allison?"

"Yes, sir?"

"Look down the hall and tell me…Mister Grainger's door — is it open or closed?"

"Closed, Mister Morrison."

"Thank you."

"Yes, sir."

Ms Almeda departed for the washroom, where she would remove — or attempt to remove — her sugar stain.

So, he thought — as he flashed the paper open to the want ads — all thoughts of brokers and sky bolts, Jaguars and dead pigeons swept away by his certainty that he had discovered the source of Cynthia's larded income. *That's what she does. She gives out our number in the papers. That's how she gets her lovers. Over the telephone! Maybe Teddy Grainger doesn't even know it's her!*

But when he looked, the number wasn't there.

Although, he thought, something in the way Ms Almeda had said that Teddy Grainger found his fantasy numbers in the papers indicated she might not mean *The Globe and Mail*.

Seriously, though, he thought as he was walking out to lunch, *I should buy the other papers, just in case, and look.*

Morrison always ate alone, unless he had to wine and dine a client. His usual restaurant was a sandwich place in the local subterranean mall. But today, with all its promise of spring and all its windswept pedestrians, was just too glorious to waste by going underground. *Look at all the legs,* he said to himself as he strode along in the warm May breeze. *Look at all the legs and all the thighs....*

This was precisely when the second sky bolt fell at his feet.

That night, Morrison and Cynthia were meant to attend the all-Beethoven concert at Roy Thomson Hall.

The whole afternoon, Morrison had pored through that morning's *Sun* and the afternoon *Star.* Fantasy, fantasy, fantasy calls — he had licked his finger and run it down the columns. All to no avail. His number — Cynthia's number — wasn't there.

Still, he had the sky to think about — to worry about — and he lost all memory of its being Thursday and, therefore, concert time.

Standing in the living-room, revelling briefly in the twilight — his favourite time of day — Morrison idly fixed himself a drink and then a drink for Cynthia.

Cynthia came down the stairs and called out into the kitchen: "don't let Alexis forget to practise, Oriana. And be sure that Seiji eats all his carrots. The spots on his chin are getting worse." And then "good evening, darling," to her husband as she swept around the corner wearing a black velvet dress and a tasteful loop of diamonds.

"Yes," said Morrison — startled. This was not the figure he had expected. "Good evening, dear." He had expected her to be dressed in an open negligee — peach-coloured lace from Frederick's of Hollywood — and her lipstick smeared and a telephone in her hand and her hair undone.

They stood and talked about where they might have dinner. "Why not Ed's Warehouse?" Cynthia suggested. "It's right across the road....Did you have a good day?"

"Yes, I did," said Morrison, absently. His mind was trying very hard to catch up with this scene in which he felt he had forgotten his lines and was in danger of gross embarrassment.

He looked out the windows.

There was the forsythia — there were the Japanese cherry trees — there were the magnolias.

What — what was it he had forgotten to say? Or do?

Then his gaze slid sideways towards the driveway. There was the BMW.

Oh.

And he felt in his pockets till he'd found the keys and he threw them at his wife.

"There," he said. "That's yours."

Cynthia was overcome with gratitude.

She spilled her drink and threw her arms around his neck and kissed him right where the mouthpiece of a telephone might have rested against his chin and she clasped her hands, stepped back and said to him: "oh, my darling — you're an angel. What a perfectly lovely gift!" And then, with suitable humility: "but what will *you* be driving...?"

Morrison dabbed at her lipstick on his chin with his handkerchief and he looked out through the window. Now for his moment of triumph.

But the place beside the curb was empty.

He had forgotten to buy the Jaguar.

Everyone was waiting for the conductor — Andrew Davis — to make his entrance and begin *The Consecration of the House*. This music was — it so happened — one of Morrison's favourite compositions. Cynthia, even with the programme staring her in the face, insisted on calling it *The Conservation of the House*, as if it might be about a new coat of paint and a shingle roof. Nonetheless, whether its hymns and trumpet calls were odes to dedication or to cedar shakes, Cynthia genuinely shared her husband's enthusiasm — happily tapping out the rhythms with her fingernails — scratching whatever surface happened to be handy.

Morrison had been looking forward to this concert for weeks. His taste and his love of music were devoid of social pretensions and, although he played no instrument himself, Alexis and her cello had been brought together more at his urging than Cynthia's. Cynthia would have been satisfied with a flute or a piccolo — something more transportable and chic. But wasn't it wonderful, Morrison thought, to have a red-headed daughter bent above the cherrywood veneer of the world's most beautiful instrument. For it was the world's most beautiful instrument — the violoncello; its shape was as lush and perfect as a figure carved by Michelangelo.

For the first time that week, Morrison was relaxed. Almost relaxed. His fingers were playing with the crease in his trousers — fidgeting with his knees — but meanwhile his neck, his shoulders and his feet were at ease and he felt no strain as he waited for the music.

All the while Cynthia had been driving them downtown in her newly acquired BMW, Morrison had tried to stave off his apprehension. Somehow, it seemed imperative that nothing fall from the sky in Cynthia's presence. A sky bolt crashing through the roof of the BMW could only prove Morrison had been chosen by the gods to pay for his sins in public; a marked man, whose wife was unaware he had ever wronged society at large, or her, or their children by any deed or word. And he hadn't. Nevertheless, he had convinced himself the gods — or God — believed he had. He felt like a prisoner, wrongfully accused — standing before a judge who refused to name his crime.

What if another pigeon came hurtling through the windshield right there on University Avenue? What would Cynthia say? Perhaps he could pass it off as the act of terrorists. *I happen to know*, he could say, *the Irish ambassador drives a BMW just like this — and the Protestants are out to get him....*

With a pigeon?

No.

Even Cynthia would not believe such a thing. He would have to think of something else. An earthquake, perhaps — or the faulty architecture of the 1920s revealing its flaws at last, casting down stones that had been improperly aligned and balanced.

Maybe he could get away with that.

But Morrison had no need for explanations. Nothing fell. The fact was, everything was going rather well. They even found a spot for the car on King Street and thus avoided having to pay the parking lot attendant the usual ten dollars.

Dinner had been exemplary: Chateaubriand for two and a bottle of 1983 Moulin-à-Vent, followed by one of the best Napoleons Morrison had ever encountered. He had worn his new John Bulloch suit — the first time ever — in honour of Beethoven, and all through dinner he hadn't dropped a single piece of food in his lap. He hadn't even dipped his sleeve in the salad.

As they crossed the street under the full light of the moon — as well as all the lights that winked and shone like stars on the Royal Alexandra Theatre — there had not been a single incident to mar their progress. Now, here they were in their lifetime seats and the concert was about to begin.

Morrison eased himself down into the grey plush and focused on the red-headed violinist in the orchestra. There she was — the star of his childhood, the love of his youth, the unbroached subject of his fantasies — tuning her violin, wearing her black velvet dress and pretending with evident success that Morrison wasn't there. It didn't matter to him that she was unaware of his existence. Somewhere, deep in his past, he had assigned himself the role of the secret lover from afar. He knew that in every woman's dreams a lover such as he existed and he knew that, because of this, she must — at least from time to time — have sensed his presence in the audience. Once, a dozen years ago, she had looked up straight into his eyes and blushed and smiled. This had happened back in the time when the orchestra was housed at Massey Hall, and the rake of the balconies was steeper and more revealing. Tonight, she ignored him — but that didn't mean he did not exist.

Cynthia, beside him, was sliding out of her furs and draping them over her shoulders. Her perfume, agitated and warmed by this activity, gave off a burst of scent that was overwhelmingly sexual. A man behind Morrison leaned forward suddenly and offered his assistance in Cynthia's struggle with her sable.

"Thank you, kind sir," she said, rather too much the way Debbie Reynolds might have said it in a musical. Perky.

Morrison, turning only slightly, noted the man had let his finger stray over Cynthia's bared neck, lingering unnecessarily as he withdrew it up behind her ear. Morrison also noted how deep the cleavage was of Cynthia's dress and how lush her breasts appeared to be (and were) beneath the velvet.

Oh, he thought, *when will it ever end?* And he wished that she would wither and be ninety.

Sighing, Morrison made the mistake of casting his eyes at heaven.

There above him was all that glass that adorns the upper reaches of Roy Thomson Hall — its mass of acoustic chandeliers — its dome of brilliant lights. Its bombs.

Morrison was on his feet at once.

Cynthia said: "what is it?"

"Uhm," said Morrison. "Nothing. Don't move. Goodbye."

Against his will — and against all reason — he fled two steps at a time towards the rear of the balcony, all the while holding his programme over his head.

Cynthia, leaving her sable behind her, followed him — though not two steps at a time. Her heels and her sense of dignity refused to accommodate her urge to run. What could be wrong?

Clutching her little silver bag, she reached her husband and beseeched him not unlike a child.

"Tell me," she said. "What is happening? Are you ill?"

"No," said Morrison. "Yes."

"Are you going to have a heart attack?" she said. Cynthia could say such things without imputing their likelihood. She might have said *are you going to have a headache?*

"No," said Morrison. *Yes,* he said in his mind.

Then, aloud — and because the lights were flashing and the concert was about to begin — he said to Cynthia: "please. I'll be all right. It was just a sudden twitch. A spasm. I was afraid I was going to have a cramp. Go back. Sit down. I'll join you later."

"Are you sure?" said Cynthia.

"Yes," said Morrison. "Positive. Here comes Andrew Davis. Hurry."

Cynthia shrugged and said: "okay," and walked down, moving sideways — holding her breasts discreetly in place with a hand across her heart.

Andrew Davis had indeed arrived, and once the lights had dimmed, he raised both arms in the air and, after a suitable pause in which he silently gained control of time and all the expectations in the auditorium, he flung his hands out into the orchestra. Or so it seemed. His fingers flew through the air and the first of the five mighty chords with which *The Consecration of the House* begins sounded as his fingers struck the instruments: the trumpets and the drums, the violins — the cellos...

Morrison fished out his handkerchief and dabbed it over his forehead.

He regained his breath by force of will, and he told himself not to think about all the sky bolts falling from the sky and all the glass above his head. *Nothing is going to happen*, he said, inside. *We live in a civilized, ordered world and the sky doesn't fall except in fairy tales and no chandelier has fallen since the nineteenth century....*

Here was the hymn of *The Consecration of the House*. How could he be afraid in the presence of such assurance and such nobility? Morrison watched his violinist — arm and shoulder, wrist and fingers — and the bow moving in and out of the lights. Her body had become a sounding box and the music was visible, written on her face.

All the people straining forward, all the people and all their ghosts were being lifted upward — enlivened in their seats. And all the glass above them and all the glass around them was shaking silently — quivering with what appeared to be the desire to sing — throwing back the music, just as it had been designed to do, with all its baffling shapes and all its angled and refracted light.

And underneath that light, those shapes, he could see the back of Cynthia's head, its red hair delicately waved, its angle of repose decidedly intent upon the scene before it – and though he could not see her eyes, Morrison knew they would be full of tears. And there, beyond her – just beyond her, so it seemed – and touchable if only Morrison had ever achieved the courage, was the object of his spiritual lust: a woman with a violin.

Yet Cynthia, for all her tears, was cheating on him with his brother – dusting the secret places of her body with perfumes attractive to strangers – courting the world at large on her telephone (using his number!) – deserting him with all his unspoken needs, for others whose up-market boldness she could now entice from behind the wheel of her BMW.

Still, it was true that none of this was apparent – none of this was more than a passive reflection, here in the presence of the music. If only *The Consecration of the House* need not ever draw to a close.

There they all sat, the lawyers and the brokers and the psychiatrists; the university students and the university professors, the dreamers and the doers, each with a secret vice and each with a secret activity – each with a secret vocabulary of lust and provocation. Duplicity. Duplicity. If only, Morrison thought, he could join in their duplicity – then maybe he could join in their ignorance of…

What?

Of falling sky bolts; of crashing chandeliers and pigeons in the gutter?

Now, *The Consecration of the House* was nearing its end. The music had begun to dance around the orchestra, leaping from instrument to instrument. Morrison listened to its well-known and beloved patterns edging their way to resolution and he felt, all at once, a resurgence of terror.

What if, once the music ended, the applause should bring down the roof?

Surely no such thing had ever happened. And yet — if he was present, it might. After all, the sky had fallen only at his feet, not at the feet, so far, of any others.

"Run," he said out loud. And then again. "Run!"

The music all but drowned his cry and only a few heads turned.

"I beg your pardon," said the usher, who had been watching him suspiciously, wondering what to do about this man who seemed so nervous and unsure of himself. "If you speak again, I shall have to ask you to leave," he said.

But the usher need not have worried. Morrison relieved him of all responsibility by leaving of his own accord.

Out through the doors and along the corridor and down the multiple flights of stairs he fled — only praying he could reach the street before the applause began. God knew, if he could do this — run this race and win — Morrison might be able to save a thousand lives. And one. Not his own, but a toss-up between the lives of a red-haired violinist and his wife.

Later that night — much later — Morrison explained to Cynthia that some people's nervous breakdowns are best left alone, allowed to expand until the meaning of the crisis has announced itself in some definitive act.

"You mean that yelling *run!* and racing out of Roy Thomson Hall in the middle of Beethoven isn't definitive?" Cynthia shouted at him, hoarsely. She had been shouting at him ever since she had found him standing in the street. "I've never been so mortified in all my life!" she shouted. "Surely you could have waited until the piece was over!"

"No," he said. "I couldn't wait. I'm sorry." How could he explain this?

"Well, if it hadn't been for that nice, considerate man behind us, I might not have survived my walk up those stairs in the dark. He came with me all the way. And you didn't even wait in the lobby. How could you embarrass me like that? How could you do that? Why?"

"I can't explain," said Morrison. "But I will explain, if I find the answer."

"Where will you find the answer? Where? You expect to find it lying in the street?"

"Well…yes, as a matter of fact. Or, maybe."

"You're not even talking sense," said Cynthia. "And if you don't start talking sense by morning, I'm going to call Doctor Pollard. After all, we have the children to think of."

"Yes," said Morrison — weary of it all. "We have the children to think about."

Then, just as Cynthia was leaving the living-room, taking with her a tall glass of iced brandy and a box of du Maurier cigarettes, Morrison stopped her in her tracks by saying: "Who says the sky is falling?"

"What?" said Cynthia. "What did you say?" And she turned. The expression on her face was one of genuine bewilderment — as if she could not fathom his vocabulary.

"I said," said Morrison, *"who says the sky is falling?"*

"Nobody," said Cynthia.

"Yes, they do," said Morrison. "Somebody says that, somewhere."

Cynthia looked at him sideways and carefully. The wording of his question had begun to make some sense — although what kind of sense she could not yet tell.

"*Somebody* says it," Morrison continued, pouring himself a glass of scotch. He was just beginning to realize she thought he was crazy. In order to survive, he would have to take on the appearance and the tone of someone sane. And so he poured himself a drink and smiled and said to her: "I thought you might remember who it was."

"Why do you want to know?" said Cynthia — gravely suspicious.

Morrison widened his smile and said: "because the sky *is* falling, that's why."

"Chicken Little says it."

Cynthia's face was a mask of sobriety.

"Ah, yes. Chicken Little. Thank you," said Morrison.

"What do you mean the sky *is* falling?

"Just that," said Morrison. "Boom." He dropped an ice-cube onto the carpet.

Cynthia watched the cube begin to melt.

"Are you trying to tell me something?" she said.

"No," said Morrison.

"Good," said Cynthia. "I'm going to bed. Good-night." She went and stood at the bottom of the staircase — paused for a moment and then said: "I'm locking my door tonight. I'm sorry."

"That's all right," said Morrison. "I'll be locking mine, too."

Cynthia went up the stairs after that, with her ice-cubes clicking and her sable dragging behind her: the day's last kill. Morrison watched her disappear and then he drained his glass.

Afterwards, in the dark, when Cynthia had locked her door and turned out her lights, Morrison slipped on his

Aquascutum and went outside and stood on the lawn beside the forsythia bush.

There, in the night, he could smell the Japanese cherry blossoms and the cool, damp earth in the flower beds. Somewhere, way off on Yonge Street, a car gave a short, sharp bark with its horn — and a dog replied. The city rumbled in its sleep and the sky above it was full of stars.

Tomorrow, Morrison was thinking, he must not forget to buy the Jaguar. This was one of the sensible things he could now begin to do: the proof that he was sane. He would buy the Jaguar: he would start the search for a house of immense proportions in Markham, Ontario: he would instruct his broker to sell all the stock he had and he would search out markets he had never dared to broach — the forests of Brazil — the gold mines of South Africa — the shoreline of Madagascar. Cynthia would understand that he was letting go of all the repressions that had driven her away. This thing with David couldn't possibly last. Let it run its course unchecked entirely. David didn't love Cynthia; David loved women — period. And there were far too many women in the world to sacrifice them all for his brother's wife. Morrison loved Cynthia. He would have her back, he was certain. Then, he would see if he wanted to keep her.

Another thing he would do tomorrow: he would buy all the papers and he would close the door on Ms Almeda. Then, he would run his fingers up and down the columns and he would choose a number while his eyes were closed — and he would call. Maybe he would call them all.

An aeroplane — heading for Japan — was passing overhead: a jetliner out of Montreal. It was flying ahead of its sound.

Morrison wanted to turn around and run inside, but he

stood his ground. It was the bravest thing he had ever done.

Everything shook.

The lawn beneath his feet made a noise. The forsythia bush began to wave its arms. The lights of the jet began to disappear amidst the stars and the sound of its engines rolled up over the trees and the roofs around him. Morrison's ice-cubes hit the sides of his glass and he tried to steady it — placing one hand, palm down, on top of it.

He closed his eyes and forced an image of the Jaguar to appear. Inside, his children sat with their instruments — cello — violin — Seiji — Alexis. And a red-headed woman. *Oh*, he thought. *Oh*. And he almost had it — purring by the curb — and the roaring of the jet had almost passed, when the sky bolt fell.

It broke a branch of blossoms from the Japanese cherry tree.

Silently — desperately — almost dropping the glass of scotch — Morrison went and sat on the steps before his house. He sat there half an hour and wept. All he could think of was how many sky bolts might have to fall before it all let go.

Well. As he had said himself of breaking down, some events are best left alone — allowed to expand until their meaning has announced itself in some definitive act.

Whatever that might be. Whatever that might mean.

DREAMS

For R.E. Turner

Doctor Menlo was having a problem: he could not sleep and his wife — the other Doctor Menlo — was secretly staying awake in order to keep an eye on him. The trouble was that, in spite of her concern and in spite of all her efforts, Doctor Menlo — whose name was Mimi — was always nodding off because of her exhaustion.

She had tried drinking coffee, but this had no effect. She detested coffee and her system had a built-in rejection mechanism. She also prescribed herself a week's worth of Dexedrine to see if that would do the trick. *Five mg at bedtime* — all to no avail. And even though she put the plastic bottle of small orange hearts beneath her pillow and kept augmenting her intake, she would wake half an hour later with a dreadful start to discover the night was moving on to morning.

Everett Menlo had not yet declared the source of his problem. His restless condition had begun about ten days ago and had barely raised his interest. Soon, however, the time spent lying awake had increased from one to several hours and then, on Monday last, to all-night sessions. Now he lay in a state of rigid apprehension — eyes wide open, arms above his head, his hands in fists — like a man in pain unable to shut it out. His neck, his back and his shoulders constantly harried him with cramps and spasms. Everett Menlo had become a full-blown insomniac.

Clearly, Mimi Menlo concluded, her husband was refusing to sleep because he believed something dreadful was going to happen the moment he closed his eyes. She had encountered this sort of fear in one or two of her patients. Everett, on the other hand, would not discuss the subject. If the problem had been hers, he would have said *such things cannot occur if you have gained control of yourself.*

Mimi began to watch for the dawn. She would calculate its approach by listening for the increase of traffic down below the bedroom window. The Menlos' home was across the road from The Manulife Centre — corner of Bloor and Bay streets. Mimi's first sight of daylight always revealed the high, white shape of its terraced storeys. Their own apartment building was of a modest height and colour — twenty floors of smoky glass and polished brick. The shadow of the Manulife would crawl across the bedroom floor and climb the wall behind her, grey with fatigue and cold.

The Menlo beds were an arm's length apart, and lying like a rug between them was the shape of a large, black dog of unknown breed. All night long, in the dark of his well, the dog would dream and he would tell the content of his dreams the way that victims in a trance will tell of being pursued by posses of their nameless fears. He whimpered, he cried and sometimes he howled. His legs and his paws would jerk and flail and his claws would scrabble desperately against the parquet floor. Mimi — who loved this dog — would lay her hand against his side and let her fingers dabble in his coat in vain attempts to soothe him. Sometimes, she had to call his name in order to rouse him from his dreams because his heart would be racing. Other times, she smiled and thought: *at least there's one of us getting some sleep.* The dog's name was Thurber and he dreamed in beige and white.

Everett and Mimi Menlo were both psychiatrists. His field was schizophrenia; hers was autistic children. Mimi's venue was the Parkin Institute at the University of Toronto; Everett's was the Queen Street Mental Health Centre. Early in their marriage they had decided never to work as a team and not — unless it was a matter of financial life and death — to accept employment in the same institution. Both had always worked with the kind of physical intensity that kills, and yet they gave the impression this was the only tolerable way in which to function. It meant there was always a sense of peril in what they did, but the peril — according to Everett — made their lives worth living. This, at least, had been his theory twenty years ago when they were young.

Now, for whatever unnamed reason, peril had become his enemy and Everett Menlo had begun to look and behave and lose his sleep like a haunted man. But he refused to comment when Mimi asked him what was wrong. Instead, he gave the worst of all possible answers a psychiatrist can hear who seeks an explanation of a patient's silence: he said there was *absolutely nothing wrong.*

"You're sure you're not coming down with something?"

"Yes."

"And you wouldn't like a massage?"

"I've already told you: no."

"Can I get you anything?"

"No."

"And you don't want to talk?"

"That's right."

"Okay, Everett…"

"Okay, what?"

"Okay, nothing. I only hope you get some sleep tonight."

Everett stood up. "Have you been spying on me, Mimi?"

"What do you mean by *spying?*"

"Watching me all night long."

"Well, Everett, I don't see how I can fail to be aware you aren't asleep when we share this bedroom. I mean — I can hear you grinding your teeth. I can see you lying there wide awake."

"When?"

"All the time. You're staring at the ceiling."

"I've never stared at the ceiling in my whole life. I sleep on my stomach."

"You sleep on your stomach *if* you sleep. But you have not been sleeping. Period. No argument."

Everett Menlo went to his dresser and got out a pair of clean pyjamas. Turning his back on Mimi, he put them on.

Somewhat amused at the coyness of this gesture, Mimi asked what he was hiding.

"Nothing!" he shouted at her.

Mimi's mouth fell open. Everett never yelled. His anger

wasn't like that; it manifested itself in other ways, in silence and withdrawal, never shouts.

Everett was staring at her defiantly. He had slammed the bottom drawer of his dresser. Now he was fumbling with the wrapper of a pack of cigarettes.

Mimi's stomach tied a knot.

Everett hadn't touched a cigarette for weeks.

"Please don't smoke those," she said. "You'll only be sorry if you do."

"And you," he said, "will be sorry if I don't."

"But, dear..." said Mimi.

"Leave me for Christ's sake alone!" Everett yelled.

Mimi gave up and sighed and then she said: "all right. Thurber and I will go and sleep in the living-room. Goodnight."

Everett sat on the edge of his bed. His hands were shaking.

"Please," he said — apparently addressing the floor. "Don't leave me here alone. I couldn't bear that."

This was perhaps the most chilling thing he could have said to her. Mimi was alarmed; her husband was genuinely terrified of something and he would not say what it was. If she had not been who she was — if she had not known what she knew — if her years of training had not prepared her to watch for signs like this, she might have been better off. As it was, she had to face the possibility the strongest, most sensible man on earth was having a nervous breakdown of major proportions. Lots of people have breakdowns, of course; but not, she had thought, the gods of reason.

"All right," she said — her voice maintaining the kind of calm she knew a child afraid of the dark would appreciate. "In a minute I'll get us something to drink. But first, I'll go and change...."

Mimi went into the sanctum of the bathroom, where her nightgown waited for her — a portable hiding-place hanging on the back of the door. "You stay there," she said to Thurber, who had padded after her. "Mama will be out in just a moment."

Even in the dark, she could gauge Everett's tension. His shadow — all she could see of him — twitched from time to time and the twitching took on a kind of lurching rhythm, something like the broken clock in their living-room.

Mimi lay on her side and tried to close her eyes. But her eyes were tied to a will of their own and would not obey her. Now she, too, was caught in the same irreversible tide of sleeplessness that bore her husband backward through the night. Four or five times she watched him lighting cigarettes — blowing out the matches, courting disaster in the bedclothes — conjuring the worst of deaths for the three of them: a flaming pyre on the twentieth floor.

All this behaviour was utterly unlike him; foreign to his code of disciplines and ethics; alien to everything he said and believed. *Openness, directness, sharing of ideas, encouraging imaginative response to every problem. Never hide troubles. Never allow despair...* These were his directives in everything he did. Now, he had thrown them over.

One thing was certain. She was not the cause of his sleeplessness. She didn't have affairs and neither did he. He might be ill — but whenever he'd been ill before, there had been no trauma; never a trauma like this one, at any rate. Perhaps it was something about a patient — one of his tougher cases; a wall in the patient's condition they could not break through; some circumstance of someone's lack of progress — a sudden veering towards a catatonic state, for instance — something that Everett had not foreseen that had stymied him and was slowly...what? Destroying his sense of professional control? His self-esteem? His scientific certainty? If only he would speak.

Mimi thought about her own worst case: a child whose obstinant refusal to communicate was currently breaking her heart and, thus, her ability to help. If ever she had needed Everett to talk to, it was now. All her fellow doctors were locked in a battle over this child; they wanted to take him away from her. Mimi refused to give him up; he might as well have been her own flesh and blood. Everything had been done — from gentle holding sessions to violent bouts of manufactured anger — in her attempt to make the child react. She was staying with him every day from the moment he was roused to the moment he was induced to sleep with drugs.

His name was Brian Bassett and he was eight years old. He sat on the floor in the furthest corner he could achieve in one of the observation-isolation rooms where all the autistic children were placed when nothing else in their treatment — nothing of love or expertise — had managed to break their silence. Mostly, this was a signal they were coming to the end of life.

There in his four-square, glass-box room, surrounded by all that can tempt a child if a child can be tempted — toys and food and story-book companions — Brian Bassett was in the process, now, of fading away. His eyes were never closed and his arms were restrained. He was attached to three machines that nurtured him with all that science can offer. But of course, the spirit and the will to live cannot be fed by force to those who do not want to feed.

Now, in the light of Brian's Bassett's utter lack of willing contact with the world around him — his utter refusal to

111

communicate — Mimi watched her husband through the night. Everett stared at the ceiling, lit by the Manulife building's distant lamps, borne on his back further and further out to sea. She had lost him, she was certain.

When, at last, he saw that Mimi had drifted into her own and welcome sleep, Everett rose from his bed and went out into the hall, past the simulated jungle of the solarium, until he reached the dining-room. There, all the way till dawn, he amused himself with two decks of cards and endless games of Dead Man's Solitaire.

Thurber rose and shuffled after him. The dining-room was one of Thurber's favourite places in all his confined but privileged world, for it was here — as in the kitchen — that from time to time a hand descended filled with the miracle of food. But whatever it was that his master was doing up there above him on the table-top, it wasn't anything to do with feeding or with being fed. The playing cards had an old and dusty dryness to their scent and they held no appeal for the dog. So he once again lay down and .he took up his dreams, which at least gave his paws some exercise. This way, he failed to hear the advent of a new .dimension to his master's problem. This occurred precisely at 5:45 A.M. when the telephone rang and Everett Menlo, having rushed to answer it, waited breathless for a minute while he listened and then said: "yes" in a curious, strangulated fashion. Thurber — had he been awake — would have recognized in his master's voice the signal for disaster.

For weeks now, Everett had been working with a patient who was severely and uniquely schizophrenic. This patient's name was Kenneth Albright, and while he was deeply suspicious, he was also oddly caring. Kenneth Albright loved the detritus of life, such as bits of woolly dust and wads of discarded paper. He loved all dried-up leaves that had drifted from their parent trees and he loved the dead bees that had curled up to die along the window-sills of his ward. He also loved the spiderwebs seen high up in the corners of the rooms where he sat on plastic chairs and ate with plastic spoons.

Kenneth Albright talked a lot about his dreams. But his dreams had become, of late, a major stumbling block in the process of his recovery. Back in the days when Kenneth had first become Doctor Menlo's patient, the dreams had been overburdened with detail: "over-cast," as he would say, "with characters" and over-produced, again in Kenneth's phrase, "as if I were dreaming the dreams of Cecil B. de Mille."

Then he had said: "but a person can't really dream someone else's dreams. Or can they, Doctor Menlo?"

"No" had been Everett's answer − definite and certain.

Everett Menlo had been delighted, at first, with Kenneth Albright's dreams. They had been immensely entertaining − complex and filled with intriguing detail. Kenneth him-self was at a loss to explain the meaning of these dreams, but as Everett had said, it wasn't Kenneth's job to explain. That was Everett's job. His job and his pleasure. For quite a long while, during these early sessions, Everett had written out the dreams, taken them home and recounted them to Mimi.

Kenneth Albright was a paranoid schizophrenic. Four times now, he had attempted suicide. He was a fiercely angry man at times − and at other times as gentle and as pleasant as a docile child. He had suffered so greatly, in the very worst moments of his disease, that he could no longer

113

work. His job — it was almost an incidental detail in his life and had no importance for him, so it seemed — was returning reference books, in the Metro Library, to their places in the stacks. Sometimes — mostly late of an afternoon — he might begin a psychotic episode of such profound dimensions that he would attempt his suicide right behind the counter and even once, in the full view of everyone, while riding in the glass-walled elevator. It was after this last occasion that he was brought, in restraints, to be a resident patient at the Queen Street Mental Health Centre. He had slashed his wrists with a razor — but not before he had also slashed and destroyed an antique copy of *Don Quixote*, the pages of which he pasted to the walls with blood.

For a week thereafter, Kenneth Albright — just like Brian Bassett — had refused to speak or to move. Everett had him kept in an isolation cell, force-fed and drugged. Slowly, by dint of patience, encouragement and caring even Kenneth could recognize as genuine, Everett Menlo had broken through the barrier. Kenneth was removed from isolation, pampered with food and cigarettes, and he began relating his dreams.

At first there seemed to be only the dreams and nothing else in Kenneth's memory. Broken pencils, discarded toys and the telephone directory all had roles to play in these dreams but there were never any people. All the weather was bleak and all the landscapes were empty. Houses, motor cars and office buildings never made an appearance. Sounds and smells had some importance; the wind would blow, the scent of unseen fires was often described. Stairwells were plentiful, leading nowhere, all of them rising from a subterranean world that Kenneth either did not dare to visit or would not describe.

The dreams had little variation, one from another. The themes had mostly to do with loss and with being lost. The broken pencils were all given names and the discarded toys were given to one another as companions. The telephone books were the sources of recitations — hours and hours of repeated names and numbers, some of which — Everett had noted with surprise — were absolutely accurate.

All of this held fast until an incident occurred one morning that changed the face of Kenneth Albright's schizophrenia forever; an incident that stemmed — so it seemed — from something he had dreamed the night before.

Bearing in mind his previous attempts at suicide, it will be obvious that Kenneth Albright was never far from sight at the Queen Street Mental Health Centre. He was, in fact, under constant observation; constant, that is, as human beings and modern technology can manage. In the ward to which he was ultimately consigned, for instance, the toilet cabinets had no doors and the shower-rooms had no locks. Therefore, a person could not ever be alone with water, glass or shaving utensils. (All the razors were cordless automatics.) Scissors and knives were banned, as were pieces of string and rubber bands. A person could not even kill his feet and hands by binding up his wrists or ankles. Nothing poisonous was anywhere available. All the windows were barred. All the double doors between this ward and the corridors beyond were doors with triple locks and a guard was always near at hand.

Still, if people want to die, they will find a way. Mimi Menlo would discover this to her everlasting sorrow with

Brian Bassett. Everett Menlo would discover this to his everlasting horror with Kenneth Albright.

On the morning of April 19th, a Tuesday, Everett Menlo, in the best of health, had welcomed a brand-new patient into his office. This was Anne Marie Wilson, a young and brilliant pianist whose promising career had been halted mid-flight by a schizophrenic incident involving her ambition. She was, it seemed, no longer able to play and all her dreams were shattered. The cause was simple, to all appearances: Anne Marie had a sense of how, precisely, the music should be and she had not been able to master it accordingly. "Everything I attempt is terrible," she had said — in spite of all her critical accolades and all her professional success. Other doctors had tried and failed to break the barriers in Anne Marie, whose hands had taken on a life of their own, refusing altogether to work for her. Now it was Menlo's turn and hope was high.

Everett had been looking forward to his session with this prodigy. He loved all music and had thought to find some means within its discipline to reach her. She seemed so fragile, sitting there in the sunlight, and he had just begun to take his first notes when the door flew open and Louise, his secretary, had said: "I'm sorry, Doctor Menlo. There's a problem. Can you come with me at once?"

Everett excused himself.

Anne Marie was left in the sunlight to bide her time. Her fingers were moving around in her lap and she put them in her mouth to make them quiet.

Even as he'd heard his secretary speak, Everett had known the problem would be Kenneth Albright. Something in Kenneth's eyes had warned him there was trouble on the way: a certain wariness that indicated all was not as placid as it should have been, given his regimen of drugs. He had stayed long hours in one position, moving his fingers over his thighs as if to dry them on his trousers; watching his fellow patients come and go with abnormal interest — never, however, rising from his chair. An incident was on the horizon and Everett had been waiting for it, hoping it would not come.

Louise had said that Doctor Menlo was to go at once to Kenneth Albright's ward. Everett had run the whole way. Only after the attendant had let him in past the double doors, did he slow his pace to a hurried walk and wipe his brow. He didn't want Kenneth to know how alarmed he had been.

Coming to the appointed place, he paused before he entered, closing his eyes, preparing himself for whatever he might have to see. *Other people have killed themselves: I've seen it often enough,* he was thinking. *I simply won't let it affect me.* Then he went in.

The room was small and white — a dining-room — and Kenneth was sitting down in a corner, his back pressed out against the walls on either side of him. His head was bowed and his legs drawn up and he was obviously trying to hide without much success. An intern was standing above him and a nurse was kneeling down beside him. Several pieces of bandaging with blood on them were scattered near Kenneth's feet and there was a white enamel basin filled with pinkish water on the floor beside the nurse.

"Morowetz," Everett said to the intern. "Tell me what has happened here." He said this just the way he posed such questions when he took the interns through the wards at examination time, quizzing them on symptoms and prognoses.

But Morowetz the intern had no answer. He was puzzled. What had happened had no sane explanation.

Everett turned to Charterhouse, the nurse.

"On the morning of April 19th, at roughly ten-fifteen, I found Kenneth Albright covered with blood," Ms Charterhouse was to write in her report. "His hands, his arms, his face and his neck were stained. I would say the blood was fresh and the patient's clothing – mostly his shirt – was wet with it. Some – a very small amount of it – had dried on his forehead. The rest was uniformly the kind of blood you expect to find free-flowing from a wound. I called for assistance and meanwhile attempted to ascertain where Mister Albright might have been injured. I performed this examination without success. I could find no source of bleeding anywhere on Mister Albright's body."

Morowetz concurred.

The blood was someone else's.

"Was there a weapon of any kind?" Doctor Menlo had wanted to know.

"No, sir. Nothing," said Charterhouse.

"And was he alone when you found him?"

"Yes, sir. Just like this in the corner."

"And the others?"

"All the patients in the ward were examined," Morowetz told him.

"And?"

"Not one of them was bleeding."

Everett said: "I see."

He looked down at Kenneth.

"This is Doctor Menlo, Kenneth. Have you anything to tell me?"

Kenneth did not reply.

Everett said: "When you've got him back in his room and tranquillized, will you call me, please?"

Morowetz nodded.

The call never came. Kenneth had fallen asleep. Either the drugs he was given had knocked him out cold, or he had opted for silence. Either way, he was incommunicado. No one was discovered bleeding. Nothing was found to indicate an accident, a violent attack, an epileptic seizure. A weapon was not located. Kenneth Albright had not a single scratch on his flesh from stem, as Everett put it, to gudgeon. The blood, it seemed, had fallen like the rain from heaven: unexplained and inexplicable.

Later, as the day was ending, Everett Menlo left the Queen Street Mental Health Centre. He made his way home on the Queen streetcar and the Bay bus. When he reached the apartment, Thurber was waiting for him. Mimi was at a goddamned meeting.

That was the night Everett Menlo suffered the first of his failures to sleep. It was occasioned by the fact that, when he wakened sometime after three, he had just been dreaming. This, of course, was not unusual — but the dream itself was perturbing. There was someone lying there, in the bright white landscape of a hospital dining-room. Whether it was a man or a woman could not be told, it was just a human body, lying down in a pool of blood.

Kenneth Albright was kneeling beside this body, pulling it open the way a child will pull a Christmas present open — yanking at its strings and ribbons, wanting only to see the contents. Everett saw this scene from several angles, never speaking, never being spoken to. In all the time he watched — the usual dream eternity — the silence was broken only by the sound of water dripping from an unseen tap. Then, Kenneth Albright rose and was covered with blood, the way he had been that morning. He stared at Doctor Menlo, looked right through him and departed. Nothing remained in the dining-room but plastic tables and plastic chairs and the bright red thing on the floor that once had been a person. Everett Menlo did not know and could not guess who this person might have been. He only knew that Kenneth Albright had left this person's body in Everett Menlo's dream.

Three nights running, the corpse remained in its place and every time that Everett entered the dining-room in the nightmare he was certain he would find out who it was. On the fourth night, fully expecting to discover he himself was the victim, he beheld the face and saw it was a stranger.

But there are no strangers in dreams; he knew that now after twenty years of practice. *There are no strangers; there are only people in disguise.*

Mimi made one final attempt in Brian Bassett's behalf to turn away the fate to which his other doctors — both medical and psychiatric — had consigned him. Not that, as a group, they had failed to expend the full weight of all they knew and all they could do to save him. One of his medical doctors — a woman whose name was Juliet Bateman — had moved a cot into his isolation room and stayed with him twenty-four hours a day for over a week. But her health had been undermined by this and when she succumbed to the Shanghai flu she removed herself for fear of infecting Brian Bassett.

The parents had come and gone on a daily basis for months in a killing routine of visits. But parents, their presence and their loving, are not the answer when a child has fallen into an autistic state. They might as well have been strangers. And so they had been advised to stay away.

Brian Bassett was eight years old — *unlucky eight*, as one of his therapists had said — and in every other way, in terms of physical development and mental capability, he had always been a perfectly normal child. Now, in the final moments of his life, he weighed a scant thirty pounds, when he should have weighed twice that much.

Brian had not been heard to speak a single word in over a year of constant observation. Earlier — long ago as seven months — a few expressions would visit his face from time to time. Never a smile — but often a kind of sneer, a passing of judgment, terrifying in its intensity. Other times, a pinched expression would appear — a signal of the shyness peculiar to autistic children, who think of light as being unfriendly.

Mimi's militant efforts in behalf of Brian had been exemplary. Her fellow doctors thought of her as *Bassett's crazy guardian angel*. They begged her to remove herself in order to preserve her health. Being wise, being practical, they saw that all her efforts would not save him. But Mimi's version of being a guardian angel was more like being a surrogate warrior: a hired gun or a samurai. Her cool determination to thwart the enemies of silence, stillness and starvation gave her strengths that even she had been unaware were hers to command.

Brian Bassett, seated in his corner on the floor, maintained a solemn composure that lent his features a kind of unearthly beauty. His back was straight, his hands were poised, his hair was so fine he looked the very picture of a spirit waiting to enter a newborn creature. Sometimes Mimi wondered if this creature Brian Bassett waited to inhabit could be human. She thought of all the animals she had ever seen in all her travels and she fell upon the image of a newborn fawn as being the most tranquil and the most in need of stillness in order to survive. If only all the natural energy and curiosity of a newborn beast could have entered into Brian Bassett, surely, they would have transformed the boy in the corner into a vibrant, joyous human being. But it was not to be.

On the 29th of April — one week and three days after Everett had entered into his crisis of insomnia — Mimi sat on the floor in Brian Bassett's isolation room, gently massaging his arms and legs as she held him in her lap.

His weight, by now, was shocking — and his skin had become translucent. His eyes had not been closed for days — for weeks — and their expression might have been carved in stone.

"Speak to me. Speak," she whispered to him as she cradled his head beneath her chin. "Please at least speak before you die."

Nothing happened. Only silence.

Juliet Bateman — wrapped in a blanket — was watching through the observation glass as Mimi lifted up Brian Bassett and placed him in his cot. The cot had metal sides — and the sides were raised. Juliet Bateman could see Brian Bassett's eyes and his hands as Mimi stepped away.

Mimi looked at Juliet and shook her head. Juliet closed her eyes and pulled her blanket tighter like a skin that might protect her from the next five minutes.

Mimi went around the cot to the other side and dragged the IV stand in closer to the head. She fumbled for a moment with the long plastic lifelines — anti-dehydrants, nutrients — and she adjusted the needles and brought them down inside the nest of the cot where Brian Bassett lay and she lifted up his arm in order to insert the tubes and bind them into place with tape.

This was when it happened — just as Mimi Menlo was preparing to insert the second tube.

Brian Bassett looked at her and spoke.

"No," he said. "Don't."

Don't meant death.

Mimi paused — considered — and set the tube aside. Then she withdrew the tube already in place and she hung them both on the IV stand.

All right, she said to Brian Bassett in her mind, *you win.*

She looked down then with her arm along the side of the cot — and one hand trailing down so Brian Bassett could touch it if he wanted to. She smiled at him and said to him: "not to worry. Not to worry. None of us is ever going to trouble you again." He watched her carefully. "Goodbye, Brian," she said. "I love you."

Juliet Bateman saw Mimi Menlo say all this and was fairly sure she had read the words on Mimi's lips just as they had been spoken.

Mimi started out of the room. She was determined now there was no turning back and that Brian Bassett was free to go his way. But just as she was turning the handle and pressing her weight against the door — she heard Brian Bassett speak again.

"Goodbye," he said.

And died.

Mimi went back and Juliet Bateman, too, and they stayed with him another hour before they turned out his lights. "Someone else can cover his face," said Mimi. "I'm not going to do it." Juliet agreed and they came back out to tell the nurse on duty that their ward had died and their work with him was over.

On the 30th of April — a Saturday — Mimi stayed home and made her notes and she wondered if and when she would weep for Brian Bassett. Her hand, as she wrote, was

123

steady and her throat was not constricted and her eyes had no sensation beyond the burning itch of fatigue. She wondered what she looked like in the mirror, but resisted that discovery. Some things could wait. Outside it rained. Thurber dreamed in the corner. Bay Street rumbled in the basement.

Everett, in the meantime, had reached his own crisis and because of his desperate straits a part of Mimi Menlo's mind was on her husband. Now he had not slept for almost ten days. *We really ought to consign ourselves to hospital beds,* she thought. Somehow, the idea held no persuasion. It occurred to her that laughter might do a better job, if only they could find it. The brain, when over-extended, gives us the most surprisingly simple propositions, she concluded. *Stop,* it says to us. *Lie down and sleep.*

Five minutes later, Mimi found herself still sitting at the desk, with her fountain pen capped and her fingers raised to her lips in an attitude of gentle prayer. It required some effort to re-adjust her gaze and re-establish her focus on the surface of the window glass beyond which her mind had wandered. Sitting up, she had been asleep.

Thurber muttered something and stretched his legs and yawned, still asleep. Mimi glanced in his direction. *We've both been dreaming,* she thought, *but his dream continues.*

Somewhere behind her, the broken clock was attempting to strike the hour of three. Its voice was dull and rusty, needing oil.

Looking down, she saw the words BRIAN BASSETT written on the page before her and it occurred to her that, without his person, the words were nothing more than extrapolations from the alphabet – something fanciful we call a "name" in the hope that, one day, it will take on meaning.

She thought of Brian Bassett with his building blocks — pushing the letters around on the floor and coming up with more acceptable arrangements: *TINA STERABBS...IAN BRETT BASS...BEST STAB the RAIN:* a sentence. He had known all along, of course, that *BRIAN BASSETT* wasn't what he wanted because it wasn't what he was. He had come here against his will, was held here against his better judgment, fought against his captors and finally escaped.

But where was here to Ian Brett Bass? Where was here to Tina Sterabbs? Like Brian Bassett, they had all been here in someone else's dreams, and had to wait for someone else to wake before they could make their getaway.

Slowly, Mimi uncapped her fountain pen and drew a firm, black line through Brian Bassett's name. *We dreamed him,* she wrote, *that's all. And then we let him go.*

Seeing Everett standing in the doorway, knowing he had just returned from another Kenneth Albright crisis, she had no sense of apprehension. All this was only as it should be. Given the way that everything was going, it stood to reason Kenneth Albright's crisis had to come in this moment. If he managed, at last, to kill himself then at least her husband might begin to sleep again.

Far in the back of her mind a carping, critical voice remarked that any such thoughts were *deeply unfeeling and verging on the barbaric.* But Mimi dismissed this voice and another part of her brain stepped forward in her defence. *I will weep for Kenneth Albright,* she thought, *when I can weep for Brian Bassett. Now, all that matters is that Everett and I survive.*

Then she strode forward and put out her hand for Everett's briefcase, set the briefcase down and helped him out of his

125

topcoat. She was playing wife. It seemed to be the thing to do.

For the next twenty minutes Everett had nothing to say, and after he had poured himself a drink and after Mimi had done the same, they sat in their chairs and waited for Everett to catch his breath.

The first thing he said when he finally spoke was: "finish your notes?"

"Just about," Mimi told him. "I've written everything I can for now." She did not elaborate. "You're home early," she said, hoping to goad him into saying something new about Kenneth Albright.

"Yes," he said. "I am." But that was all.

Then he stood up — threw back the last of his drink and poured another. He lighted a cigarette and Mimi didn't even wince. He had been smoking now three days. The atmosphere between them had been, since then, enlivened with a magnetic kind of tension. But it was a moribund tension, slowly beginning to dissipate.

Mimi watched her husband's silent torment now with a kind of clinical detachment. This was the result, she liked to tell herself, of her training and her discipline. The lover in her could regard Everett warmly and with concern, but the psychiatrist in her could also watch him as someone suffering a nervous breakdown, someone who could not be helped until the symptoms had multiplied and declared themselves more openly.

Everett went into the darkest corner of the room and sat down hard in one of Mimi's straight-backed chairs: the ones inherited from her mother. He sat, prim, like a patient in a doctor's office, totally unrelaxed and nervy; expressionless. Either he had come to receive a deadly diagnosis, or he would get a clean bill of health.

Mimi glided over to the sofa in the window, plush and red and deeply comfortable; a place to recuperate. The view — if she chose to turn only slightly sideways — was one of the gentle rain that was falling onto Bay Street. Sopping-wet pigeons huddled on the window-sill; people across the street in the Manulife building were turning on their lights.

A renegade robin, nesting in their eaves, began to sing.

Everett Menlo began to talk.

"Please don't interrupt," he said at first.

"You know I won't," said Mimi. It was a rule that neither one should interrupt the telling of a case until they had been invited to do so.

Mimi put her fingers into her glass so the ice-cubes wouldn't click. She waited.

Everett spoke — but he spoke as if in someone else's voice, perhaps the voice of Kenneth Albright. This was not entirely unusual. Often, both Mimi and Everett Menlo spoke in the voices of their patients. What was unusual, this time, was that, speaking in Kenneth's voice, Everett began to swear profusely — so profusely that Mimi was able to watch his shirt front darkening with perspiration.

"As you know," he said, "I have not been sleeping."

This was the understatement of the year. Mimi was silent.

"I have not been sleeping because — to put it in a nut-shell — I have been afraid to dream."

Mimi was somewhat startled by this. Not by the fact that Everett was afraid to dream, but only because she had just been thinking of dreams herself.

"I have been afraid to dream, because in all my dreams there have been bodies. Corpses. Murder victims."

Mimi — not really listening — idly wondered if she had been one of them.

127

"In all my dreams, there have been corpses," Everett repeated. "But I am not the murderer. Kenneth Albright is the murderer, and, up to this moment, he has left behind him fifteen bodies: none of them people I recognize."

Mimi nodded. The ice-cubes in her drink were beginning to freeze her fingers. Any minute now, she prayed, they would surely melt.

"I gave up dreaming almost a week ago," said Everett, "thinking that if I did, the killing pattern might be altered; broken." Then he said tersely; "it was not. The killings have continued...."

"How do you know the killings have continued, Everett, if you've given up your dreaming? Wouldn't this mean he had no place to hide the bodies?"

In spite of the fact she had disobeyed their rule about not speaking, Everett answered her.

"I know they are being continued because I have seen the blood."

"Ah, yes. I see."

"No, Mimi. No. You do not see. The blood is not a figment of my imagination. The blood, in fact, is the only thing not dreamed." He explained the stains on Kenneth Albright's hands and arms and clothes and he said: "It happens every day. We have searched his person for signs of cuts and gashes — even for internal and rectal bleeding. Nothing. We have searched his quarters and all the other quarters in his ward. His ward is locked. His ward is isolated in the extreme. None of his fellow patients was ever found bleeding — never had cause to bleed. There were no injuries — no self-inflicted wounds. We thought of animals. Perhaps a mouse — a rat. But nothing. Nothing. Nothing... We also went so far as to strip-search all the members of the staff who entered that ward and I, too, offered myself for this experiment. Still nothing. Nothing. No one had bled."

Everett was now beginning to perspire so heavily he removed his jacket and threw it on the floor. Thurber woke and stared at it, startled. At first, it appeared to be the beast that had just pursued him through the woods and down the road. But, then, it sighed and settled and was just a coat; a rumpled jacket lying down on the rug.

Everett said: "we had taken samples of the blood on the patient's hands — on Kenneth Albright's hands and on his clothing and we had these samples analysed. No. It was not his own blood. No, it was not the blood of an animal. No, it was not the blood of a fellow patient. No, it was not the blood of any members of the staff...."

Everett's voice had risen.

"Whose blood was it?" he almost cried. "Whose the hell was it?"

Mimi waited.

Everett Menlo lighted another cigarette. He took a great gulp of his drink.

"Well..." He was calmer now; calmer of necessity. He had to marshall the evidence. He had to put it all in order — bring it into line with reason. "Did this mean that — somehow — the patient had managed to leave the premises — do some bloody deed and return without our knowledge of it? That is, after all, the only possible explanation. Isn't it?"

Mimi waited.

"Isn't it?" he repeated.

"Yes," she said. "It's the only possible explanation."

"Except there is no way out of that place. There is absolutely no way out."

Now, there was a pause.

"But one," he added — his voice, again, a whisper.

Mimi was silent. Fearful — watching his twisted face.

"Tell me," Everett Menlo said — the perfect innocent, almost the perfect child in quest of forbidden knowledge. "Answer me this — be honest: is there blood in dreams?"

Mimi could not respond. She felt herself go pale. Her husband — after all, the sanest man alive — had just suggested something so completely mad he might as well have handed over his reason in a paper bag and said to her, *burn this*.

"The only place that Kenneth Albright goes, I tell you, is into dreams," Everett said. "That is the only place beyond the ward into which the patient can or does escape."

Another — briefer — pause.

"It is real blood, Mimi. Real. And he gets it all from dreams. *My dreams*."

They waited for this to settle.

Everett said: "I'm tired. I'm tired. I cannot bear this any more. I'm tired...."

Mimi thought, *good. No matter what else happens, he will sleep tonight.*

He did. And so, at last, did she.

Mimi's dreams were rarely of the kind that engender fear. She dreamt more gentle scenes with open spaces that did not intimidate. She would dream quite often of water and of animals. Always, she was nothing more than an observer; roles were not assigned her; often, this was sad. Somehow, she seemed at times locked out, unable to participate. These were the dreams she endured when Brian Bassett died: field trips to see him in some desert setting; underwater excursions to watch him floating amongst the seaweed. He never spoke, and, indeed, he never appeared to be aware of her presence.

That night, when Everett fell into his bed exhausted and she did likewise, Mimi's dream of Brian Bassett was the last she would ever have of him and somehow, in the dream, she knew this. What she saw was what, in magical terms, would be called a disappearing act. Brian Bassett vanished. Gone.

Sometime after midnight on May Day morning, Mimi Menlo awoke from her dream of Brian to the sound of Thurber thumping the floor in a dream of his own.

Everett was not in his bed and Mimi cursed. She put on her wrapper and her slippers and went beyond the bedroom into the hall.

No lights were shining but the street lamps far below and the windows gave no sign of stars.

Mimi made her way past the jungle, searching for Everett in the living-room. He was not there. She would dream of this one day; it was a certainty.

"Everett?"

He did not reply.

Mimi turned and went back through the bedroom.

"Everett?"

She heard him. He was in bathroom and she went in through the door.

"Oh," she said, when she saw him. "Oh, my God."

Everett Menlo was standing in the bathtub, removing his

131

pyjamas. They were soaking wet, but not with perspiration. They were soaking wet with blood.

For a moment, holding his jacket, letting its arms hang down across his belly and his groin, Everett stared at Mimi, blank-eyed from his nightmare.

Mimi raised her hands to her mouth. She felt as one must feel, if helpless, watching someone burn alive.

Everett threw the jacket down and started to remove his trousers. His pyjamas, made of cotton, had been green. His eyes were blinded now with blood and his hands reached out to find the shower taps.

"Please don't look at me," he said. "I...Please go away."

Mimi said: "no." She sat on the toilet seat. "I'm waiting here," she told him, "until we both wake up."

THE NAME'S THE SAME

This man answered the door. When I asked for my brother he made a sort of face. I got this feeling right away that he didn't like my brother — that my brother's name wasn't very honourable around there. I felt funny.

But it was my name too.

That thought kept coming to me as I began up the staircase. "It's your name too — it is your name too."

It was a long climb to my brother's room — second floor from the top. I'd been there before — you wanted an oxygen mask the last few flights — it's the truth — you did. I got there all right, though.

He was out.

But Katie was there. Katie was Bud's fiancée.

"Bud's decided to wait for the last one. How are ya, sweetie?"

She kissed me.

"Fine. Tired — but O.K. I brought a surprise."

"Show me."

It was a bottle of cognac. I forgot to tell you we're all practically alcoholics — except me — I'm a weekend drinker. I like it. But in my work you can't afford to drink or people talk.

Anyway.

Katie took the bottle and said we'd save it till Bud got back. I took a look around.

I wish I could describe that room to you — I really do. This was a "good" house — you know, they had a Lady on the ground floor — a real lady, capital *L*. She was always making complaints, especially about Bud — but old Kitty (that was the landlady), old Kitty was as mad as a hatter and she used to come in to listen to Bud's radio all the time — so she never paid any attention to Lady Whatsit's complaints about Bud. This Lady Whatsit — god, she had a voice you could hear in Dawson City, if you know where that is. But I never saw her — Lady Whatsit I mean. She moved out later on.

But about this room of Bud's. It was like a showroom in a museum or somewhere like that. The corners were so far away and the ceiling was so high, you practically had an echo when you talked. And all the furniture was very sort of Regency — gilt chairs and lots of brocade on the covers. And on the windows, curtains like that — brocade drapes and that white material you see through like a misty day. There was a tiny little gas fire stuck into the middle of an enormous fireplace. The mantel was ninety feet long. Rug on the floor.

The bed was like a rugby field. It even had a centre line and goal posts at either end — if you know what I mean.

Katie lived in a room downstairs.

While we waited for Bud, Katie went on reading from this magazine she'd had when I came in — so I looked over Bud's books on the mantelpiece. Here's what he had:

The Great Gatsby by F. Scott Fitzgerald
The Case of the Moth-Eaten Mink
The Case of the Fiery Fingers
The Case of the Drowning Duck
The Case of the Grinning Gorilla

And another one — all by this Erle Stanley somebody — I don't even know his name — I never read that.

Then there were some magazines — you know, women and stuff — and a book of poetry: *Other Men's Flowers*. It's an anthology. Lord Wavell put it together. And a copy of Voltaire's *Candide*. (I gave him that.) That was all.

And in this cupboard (this cupboard was the only Victorian piece of furniture in the whole room) Bud put all his bottles. I wish you could have seen Bud's bottles. He had them all lined up like we used to line up our lead soldiers when we were kids. All the ones that looked alike in the same row — with an officer in front. All his officers were quart bottles of gin. He even had a whole platoon of these officers. Some army. Lousy with brass.

I was in the middle of counting them (I got to thirty, no kidding) when Katie finished her magazine.

"I'm going to put on the sausages now. He shouldn't be long — it's past closing time."

"O.K. Does this radio work?"

"Sure. It's on a battery. I just bought a new one yesterday. See if you can get Luxembourg."

She went out to cook on this little stove in the bathroom. There was only the bath and the sink in there — and this little stove and a little ice-box.

I turned on the radio. There was a man playing the trumpet. I'll always remember that. I sat there smoking a cigarette, listening to him. He was so sad; and I kept thinking of the bars back in Toronto — (we come from Toronto, Bud and I and Katie too — Katie even lives on the same street at home). We used to go to these bars and listen to the music. It was just like the man on the radio. And there was a pianist too, in Toronto — black and fat: a genius. Here in London you don't get that — so when I heard it on the radio from Luxembourg that night, I nearly cried. It was like hearing somebody calling "Come home." Just like that — "Come home." I had a drink of my cognac.

Then Bud came in. I was scared stiff. He had a broken bottle in his hand. Boy, was he drunk. I forgot to tell you — Bud is six feet five — so I had a right to be scared, not just because of the broken bottle.

I stood up and I didn't even say hello.

Bud sort of swore. I won't tell you what he said — but he stood there swearing the whole lousy book. It was about this bottle.

Then Katie tried to come in with the food on some plates and she had to walk under his other arm which he had up against the door-jamb. After she got in, he turned around and slammed the door.

I remember saying, right then (to myself, not aloud) — "It's your name too." It was funny, because I hadn't stopped being scared yet.

Katie put down the plates with our supper on them, and looked at Bud.

"What's the matter, darl?" She sounded very calm — but then she lived with him.

"Oh, it's that blankety-blank man downstairs," said Bud. "Always poking his blanking nose into whatever I do."

"What happened?"

"Oh, I came in and dropped the blanking wine all over everything in the hall. So he had to come out, of course, and see what had happened. Even before he had on the light he said 'Is that you, Cable?' In that English voice of his. 'Is that you, Cable?' — even before he'd even looked. I'm going down and kill him. I just came up with this bottle — I just brought it up — I'll be right back."

"No! No!"

That was me — because I was sure he would. Kill him, I mean.

"Leave me alone. I'm going down and wring his blankety neck. Lousy English voice — he called me Cable — like it was the army or something. No manners. I'll be right back."

He didn't move.

"Dinner's ready," said Katie.

"I'll be right back."

"Take off your coat — come on."

"I'm going down."

He looked at the broken bottle. "I only bought it because Neil was coming. You'd think I *wanted* to break the blanking thing. I'll be right back."

He started to go, bottle in hand.

Katie went over.

"Now you come and sit down. Did you clear up the mess?"

"Yes. Going now — "

"No!" — she was a rock — she really was.

"Going Kate — so just move off."

Well, he hit her then. She fell down.

I went over. I was flaming mad.

"Who the hell do you think you are? An animal? You're behaving like a horse. You stop it."

"Oh, I only hit her a little."

"You knocked her right down. You give me that." I grabbed for it.

"Stand back from me!"

He was really mad — and drunker than I'd thought he was.

"Now I'm going down."

I still said "No." So did Katie. Then she said, "Neil brought a present — some cognac," — and I said: "I'm not giving him that anymore," and she said: "Yes you are," and "We'll drink it instead of the wine. We'll forget about the wine," and I said: "No!" Bud said: "I don't want it — you called me a lousy animal"; and I said: "Well you are!" and Katie began to cry, and Bud said: "Who the hell are you to call your own brother an animal? You're just like that blanking major and that blankety Lady Chamber Pot. You're just a — a terrible little snob." And I said: "Blank you," and he said: "Leave," and I said: "All right, I will then"; and then Katie was through crying and said we had to stop yelling or everybody'd be upstairs so we stopped.

We looked at each other. I'll tell you right now — I really hated him then. I never wanted to see him again.

And the radio still had that man playing the trumpet.

After supper we sat around and drank the cognac. I won't tell you about all that — we kept apologizing all the time and Katie cried and I felt pretty awful about calling Bud a horse and then I started off about Bud's books.

I haven't told you that I read a lot. I read a lot of poetry and I've read nearly every good book in English — so that I really did want Bud to read something else besides Erle Stanley Whosis. I just started out to explain it all quietly — but you know what it's like when you get excited about something. I just went on and on and on about it. About how he should read Shakespeare and *Moby Dick* and *The Brothers Karamazov* and everything, so that he finally got hurt or something. He said he'd read *Candide*, but he hadn't read *Candide*, because the back was all right. Then he stood up and said: "Well, I've read that Great Gatsby book and that's F. Scott Fitzgerald. And he can write. I'd read anything he cares to write — F. Scott Fitzgerald."

And I had to go and say, "He's dead."

"I don't care — it's a good book and I read it."

And I said: "Well if you'd read more of that — O.K. — but hell — look what's on your mantelpiece. Murders and lousy dirty magazines."

"I've got *Candide!*" he shouted.

"You haven't even touched it."

"I have. I have too. It's about this boy and the best of all possible worlds."

"You just heard that from somewhere."

"I read it — I read it! And the Fitzgerald. That's there — look at it!"

He reached out at it and touched it.

It had a yellow cover.

"Well I know one thing," I said. "If F. Scott Fitzgerald came in here and saw your mantelpiece — he'd just be ashamed — that's what he'd be."

"I've read it." He was almost crying — I even think he was. God — I didn't even know what I'd done.

"Then why don't you read something else that's decent?"

"You leave me! You get out — go away! I never —" I was on the stairs by now — I was all ready to leave. "I never want to see you again — you leave me — you leave me —!"

And so I left. It was funny. Both of us forgot about *Other Men's Flowers*.

There's a lot of good stuff in that, and that was there.

Then Katie left. She went back to Canada. She went home. Bud came to see me the day after.

I guess I just didn't understand all that. He hadn't been to sleep — and he wouldn't eat what I gave him. He walked up and down in my room.

If I tell you about my room you'll think I'm a louse. Comparisons are lousy. I mean, it's just that I'd have to tell you about all my books and that. I had them all laid out in neat rows on top of everything that would take them. God, I loved those books. I dusted them everyday. I used to just sit and watch them sometimes.

Now that I have — I'm glad I told you. I guess it isn't so lousy, if you love a thing. I just wished that Bud could have loved them too. That's all.

Anyway, then he told me.

"I need some money."

"Why? Haven't you got your job?"

"No."

"Why not? Did they fire you?"

He walked up and down twice before he even answered. Then he sort of looked out the window and said: "I never had a job."

"What do you mean?"

"All that money and everything — was Katie's."

I hadn't had a clue.

I didn't say anything though. I was sort of angry and I wanted to cry too. I'm not just sure why.

And then he said: "You knew that, didn't you?"

I said no.

"Well it's true. That's the way it was. So I need some money."

I don't make much money. I have this important job I told you about — but it's more the people I meet than the money I make. So I didn't have anything to give him. Besides, I thought he should make his own.

"Can't you get a job?"

"Well, no." — the classic answer. "You see there's this chance of a trip home free — on a boat. I'd sort of work my way, you see. And that's liable to just happen any day. So I can't — I mean I just don't *dare* to take up a job I'd have to throw down in two days or something."

He could go on talking like that for hours. I've heard him. All about why he doesn't work.

He walked up and down.

"I can give you a pound," I said.

"Ah, thanks Neil — that's terrific, boy — really it is."

I gave it to him.

"But what'll you do when that's gone?"

"I'll go down to Dad's office tomorrow and borrow some from old Davies."

My father's firm had a sort of branch in all the world capitals.

Then he said he'd go now, because he was tired and hadn't slept since Katie left. He was really lonesome for her too — you could tell. I gave him some canned food and some cigarettes. I tried to make him take that other Scott Fitzgerald book, *Tender Is the Night*, but he said he was too tired to read. He wanted my old magazines, though. He'd look at the pictures. I was sort of sorry, even, that I didn't have any of those men's magazines with the women in them. I didn't really care about him not taking *Tender Is the Night* because he was so lonely, pictures would be easier. I didn't see him after that for a long time. Weeks even.

Then it was his birthday. He was twenty-six. Still no job. He must have made a big touch on Mr Davies. And then Katie was always writing to him – and she'd sent some money too.

I phoned him up and said I'd take him for a birthday party – a good meal. To a restaurant. I thought he'd like that. I wanted him to have a steak – not because steak was his favourite or anything, but because it made a nice picture; Bud eating steak.

But he wanted to have a drink instead. We'd go somewhere quiet and talk. His boat would come soon and he wanted to say goodbye in case he had to leave in a hurry. This boat was always coming. I don't even know what name it had.

So I gave up the steak idea and we went out and got sort of drunk. I bought him a bottle of gin to take away with him and got in a taxi. I felt suddenly so old. Older even than Bud – and of course, he's older than me – way older.

I gave him two pounds. I wasn't drunk any more; I just gave it to him because I kept hearing these two things over and over in my brain. "It's your name too," was one of them and the other was, "If Scott Fitzgerald came in here and saw your mantelpiece he'd just be ashamed."

Well, I meant to leave him at his place and go on home alone. But I couldn't. I got out of the taxi with him and he invited me up for a drink of that gin I'd bought.

The house was all dark – they hadn't even left the light

144

on in the hall for him. I remembered the last time I came.

He went first. I went second.

The first thing I noticed was how bad his breathing was — really bad, like a man with asthma or something like that. Then I hung back so that I could watch him going up in front of me. He was all bent over and all the way up he kept talking in between these very noisy breaths.

He kept calling me Katie by mistake, and kid and boy and "Neil-hopper."

"Neil-hopper" was a name I had when we were children but I've forgotten why.

And he looked so bent over and his coat was all undone and it made him look like an old man with some sort of sickness.

We got to his floor — but we didn't turn off. "I forgot to tell you," he said, "Kittyhawk put me up in the cheap room." He laughed.

Cheap room! You should have been there!

He went in first and turned on the light. It was just a bulb to one side of this old window.

There wasn't any cupboard for the army, so they were all lined up on the hearth. He told me which ones to use for ashtrays. Special ones — plain glass so that you could see inside. He didn't light the gas fire at all. When he went out I put some money in and lit it up. It was really cold in that room. Icelandia. Icelandia was a skating rink at home.

But he didn't go out just yet. He put his coat on this very tatty Victorian sofa and told me to put mine there too. I looked around a bit. It was all neat — but there were no rugs and the eiderdown was lumpy and the bedspread had a hole right in the middle and there was a bit of old green stuff — dead — left over from Christmas, months ago. He'd put it in one of the officers on a table. There was a picture postcard too — one that I'd sent him from somewhere. He had it on the mantelpiece — all alone.

Then he went out. When he went by me I saw his shoes. They were as clean as a whistle. And do you know what else? His shirt was clean too. I couldn't get over that. He looked much neater and even cleaner than I did. Self respect.

It began to get warm. I turned on the radio but the battery was dead and you couldn't get Luxembourg any more. You couldn't even get London.

Then he came back.

"If you hit it on top you get music."

I hit it — the radio — and you could just hear it, far, far away.

I went to turn it off.

"Leave it on," he said "Please. I like to hear it."

"But you *can't* hear it," I said.

"Yes I can. I can hear it."

He gave me some gin in a pink plastic cup he'd stolen from the bathroom.

We just sat.

I looked around a bit more — not too carefully. I knew he'd know I was looking for books. But I could tell there weren't any.

And this is the hard part now. I mean I can't explain it at all. But I just started to cry. I cried. I cried from way down inside — you know, where it hurts you to cry. And I couldn't stop. I tried — but I couldn't.

It was crazy. I can't describe it — but suddenly this something came up inside me and I kept remembering everything I'd said to him and thought about him. And I felt like — I don't know — a heel I guess, because (I don't know why) but I kept thinking that it was my fault that he was living like that — in that awful room and I just hated it.

146

And then I suddenly thought that he just didn't realize —
he didn't have any idea at all, about how lousy I am and
what a fraud I was and how I'd really meant it when I
called him a horse. That was when I remembered the
postcard — on the mantel all by itself — from me.

And then I saw this bit of paper — it was just lying on the
floor, to keep the bottle that was on it from marking the
boards, I guess. And I saw what he'd written there — over
and over again in ink.

He'd written out — "Sir Thomas Cable — Bart." (that was
his real name — Thomas) "Sir Thomas Cable — Bart." all in
writing over and over on this bit of old paper to keep the
floor clean.

Well — that's sort of when I understood. I wish I could
explain it better — but I can't, because I'm not too sure just
what it really means. But I know that I understood it — and
I still do. All I have to do is say it over to myself and then I
understand.

"Sir Thomas Cable — Bart."

I guess you ought to know — I haven't seen him since.
I've wanted to — really I have — but I'm not the same any
more. I go on reading my books — but I'm not the same.
And I think about him — I think about him all the time.

But I can't. I just can't face it again, that room and the
bottles and my postcard and that piece of paper — and
Luxembourg.

I wish he'd come to see me. But he won't. I guess he has
real pride. You know — "Sir Thomas Cable — Bart." That
sort of thing.

REAL LIFE WRITES
REAL BAD

I had an accident, once, and my dog was killed. This was a long time ago. I'd been riding my bike and the dog, whose name was Danny, had been running along beside me on the road. It was a country road and there was a lot of dust because it hadn't rained. A truck came by and it knocked me off my bike and Danny went under the wheels and he disappeared. The truck drove on and Danny's body went on with it.

Bud, my brother, came running — I don't remember where he'd been. I refused to leave the side of the road. My arm was fractured and my legs were pitted with gravel and they were bleeding — but this was nothing compared to my grief and the shock of Danny's disappearance. "I won't go home without him," I said. "I'd rather stay here and die."

Bud said: "Okay, Neil. I'll go and get him." Just like that: an everyday occurrence.

One whole hour he was gone. I remember that afternoon precisely — every detail. I crouched beside the road and I brushed away the flies that were coming after my legs and I kept my eye on the long, hot road where Bud had gone out of sight beyond a railroad track. The heat — it was July 15th — made waves in the air and I think I was close to fainting when I finally saw him coming back.

I swear I saw him growing before my eyes, that day. He was like a man we had seen unfolding from a box at the circus, once. The box had been collapsed with the man inside and when the magician waved his wand, the box was whole again and the man came out. And that was Bud that afternoon. A miracle.

He was carrying Danny, dead, in his arms and he said: "We can go now. I found him." The dog had been lying in a ditch full of water, two miles down the road. I guess the driver had thrown him there.

We left my broken bike behind and we went back home to where our mother was waiting. It wasn't really home, but a farm where we'd been staying. This was the summer of 1941 when our dad was in the army and Bud was twelve and I was ten.

"Danny is dead," Bud told our mother. "But this dog's alive." He put his hand on my head and smiled.

Bud thought — even then — that each scene had to have its tag-line. *This dog is dead*, Errol Flynn had said in *Captain Farrago. But this dog is still alive....*

In spite of all that's happened since and all the hell he's

put us through, I often recall the image of Bud unfolding along the road that afternoon, as if the magician had waved his wand and out had stepped my brother — whole — with Danny in his arms.

He might have thought he was Errol Flynn; who cares? To me, it's the only image I have of Bud the way he was before his dreams took over; the ones about the end of time and the ones about the box before it was collapsed.

I guess we were all expecting it — all of us prepared for the worst — but everyone praying it wouldn't happen yet. This is what they call the Scarlett O'Hara syndrome. You know the one: *I'll think about that tomorrow.* The only trouble is, in real life, tomorrow has a funny way of turning up today.

Bud always had a love of books and a prodigious memory. The two, when combined, produced his unpleasant habit of dropping acid quotes into life's worst moments. Bud was the one who was always there to remind you how many times he'd told you not to play with matches, just when you'd burned the house down.

Sadly, he wasn't good at using this fund of plagiarized wisdom when it came to himself. For instance, the day we found him, a piece of paper was discovered — by the telephone — on which Bud had carefully written out for someone else's benefit a poem by Dorothy Parker. Here it is — but you have to imagine Bud's handwritten version of it, the way he made all the letters perfect because he was so afraid he'd lost his powers of concentration. In the margin he had written: *Hartley — 484 9842 — April 2.* And then:

> *Razors pain you;*
> *Rivers are damp;*

Acids stain you;
And drugs cause cramp.
Guns aren't lawful;
Nooses give;
Gas smells awful;
You might as well live.

Bud's oldest friend, Teddy Hartley, killed himself on April 9th.

It may well be that I'm maligning Bud by saying he never applied his found advice to himself. All I have to go on is my witness. And my witness was that Bud ignored all good advice — the way most desperadoes do — until it was too late. Maybe, on the other hand — just before his brain burned out — he did remember what he'd written down on that piece of paper for Teddy Hartley. And maybe it made him want to live. I'll never know, but my guess would be — it made him laugh.

Was Bud, my brother, a true desperado?

Yes; I think he was. He lived his life strung out as far away from reality as he could get. Back when he was twenty-seven, Bud decided life had been best when he was twenty-six. Time must be made to stop if he was going to survive. And so he chose to live in a world rendered timeless by alcohol.

Bud was a destructive man and people turned away from

him in droves. He wasn't easy to take; he came, almost, to delight in driving you away. When I add up all there is to say, I'd have to say I didn't like my brother, Bud. I loved him, though.

If I had been a writer and if Bud had been a person in a story, this is where, in that story, there would be a description of Bud before the fall, in all his glory. That way, in stories, writers justify their failing heroes. The trouble is, Bud had no glory. What he had, instead, was anti-glory: fear and rage and disappointment.

All his life, Bud wanted out of being who he was. It wasn't so much that he hated being Thomas "Bud" Cable as the fact that Thomas "Bud" Cable hadn't been given "the breaks." Everyone else, according to Bud, had been given something at birth that made for an easy passage. Money, looks and talent were the main things he lacked. He also lacked what he called "a name to go by," meaning he might have managed getting by if his name, at birth, had been John Paul Getty.

Bud never knew this was funny, by the way. Once he retired from the world he never got the chance to see that everyone else might want a different birthright than the one they had. That even Errol Flynn might want to be Cary Grant.

Katie, Bud's wife, once asked him why he didn't go out and make his own fortune "instead of hanging around the house waiting for the money tree to bloom."

Bud said he couldn't do that.

"Why not?" said Katie. "Everybody else does."

"I know," said Bud. "But it takes them so *long*...."

When Katie told me this, I laughed out loud and said: "so much for money!"

"No," said Katie, "so much for work."

Bud not only wanted out of who he was, he wanted out of his body, too. He would stand in front of mirrors and curse the elongation of his bones.

"Look at my head," he would say, his voice always rising up the scale and getting louder. "Look at the shape of my fucking head! It's like a goddamned shoe box!" he'd yell. "A goddamned shoe box and the fucking shoes inside are goddamned size fourteen!"

Every time he looked, you might have thought he'd never seen himself in mirrors or photographs before. He was constantly appalled and panic-stricken by what he saw. He always cringed while peering at himself through narrowed eyes — a voyeur watching through a window. "Look at his hands!" he would say, as if the person in the mirror wasn't him. "Look at the size of his bloody hands, Neil!"

This much was true: Bud stood so tall he had to crouch when passing through doorways, reaching up with his fingers to protect the top of his head. He stooped wherever he went and he even stooped when he was lying down — his middle caved, his legs drawn up, his back an arabesque. All his clothes were bought at what he called The Grotesquery on King Street East — a store for oversized men and women. Katie had to do the shopping. Bud had gone there once, but the size of the exaggerated mannikins had traumatized him. "I don't really look like that," he kept repeating. "Tell me I don't really look like that...." He didn't, of course, but nothing would persuade him of it.

He told me, once, he'd had a dream in which there was a spa for the oversized. "They can perform an operation there where they saw your bones in half," he said. "You go

156

to sleep and wake up two feet shorter!" There were also magic baths in which you steamed your height away. *Contraction Waters*, they were called. *Shrinkage guaranteed!*

But the best thing of all, Bud said, was the fact they had "a magic shampoo for reducing the size of shoe-box heads...."

It was sad, I guess. Bud didn't like to walk in the streets. He became alarmed when the prospect opened up that he might be asked to meet a stranger. "What will they say," he would ask, "when they see me?"

Somehow, it never occurred to him they might just say *hello*.

During Bud's early revels, Katie would join him, lending her sense of fun to everything he did. She withdrew only when, at last, it came to be obvious that Bud had no intention of stopping. Ever. It took until they were in their early forties for this to happen — not until their money was running out and their friends had begun to turn down their invitations. The trouble was, Bud showed no inclination to believe that either dwindling funds or loss of friends had anything to do with how much he drank.

Neither was he inclined to support his drinking habit by getting a job. I'm talking about the early-to-mid-1970s here, and Bud had not set foot inside the workplace since 1962 when, for a month, he had answered a telephone somewhere downtown for one of those fly-by-night firms that used to sell household cleaning products after midnight on television. Bud, in fact, didn't answer anything. He listened to a recording device on which the potential customers were meant to leave their names and addresses. The reason he quit this job, so he told me at length in one of his endless monologues, was because so many of the recorded phone calls were obscene. *The world*, he informed me, *is a rotten apple and to hell with it!*

Bud was a man who could deliver a two-hour tirade on almost any given subject, drop of a hat. His diatribes were unencumbered by reason and as time went on they became his only mode of conversation. Increasingly, the focus of these harangues was reality itself — though Bud, of course, would never have called it that. He would have called it *the great conspiracy* or *the universal menace* or *the sinister intruder*. Reality was anything — or anyone — that challenged the rightness of Bud's withdrawal from society. It was, of course, a psychotic withdrawal — but those who loved him, myself included, refused to see that. To us, Bud must not be thought of as insane — because he must always be seen as someone who, having gone astray, could return to the fold through an act of will. Our mother was always saying this in Bud's behalf. *His reason will bring him back to us,* she'd say. *He only needs to come to his senses and exercise his will.* But alcohol — if not the alcoholic — repudiates the will. It has no tolerance for anything connected with the self.

This way, as Bud went all the way downhill and finally took up residence at the bottom, I, too, became less tolerant of reality. I only mean where Bud was concerned. Reality was so predictable. It operated entirely without imagination. It might as well have been a textbook. Besides which, it had such bad taste. Imagine Thomas Cable, Jr. — Bud — ensconced in his suit and tie — his shoes highly polished — his hair and his fingernails impeccable — sitting in his darkened living-room at noon with his bottles of Beaujolais at hand — raising his glass to his lips and his gaze upon the flickering screen that has become his only companion.

"What are you watching?" I ask, when I telephone.

"*Roger Ramjet,*" Bud informs me. "Don't interrupt me, now. I'll talk to you later on."

And he hangs up.

This was Bud, aged fifty-four.

When Katie died, I had to tell him over and over she was gone and in the grave. He simply did not believe me. Not because he was obtuse — (perhaps the alcohol was obtuse) — but because the image of Katie dead could not be made to fit into what he thought was reality. Death was not proper. It couldn't just walk in like that and take up residence. Bud had not accounted for it in his scheme of things.

He refused to come to the lying-in. He said it was a put-up job.

"You're lying, Neil," he said to me. "You're only trying to protect her because you've always taken her side in everything...."

"No, Bud," I'd say to him — (we had this conversation at least four times) — "Katie had cancer and died."

He would look at me then, as if I was a traitor. Katie wasn't dead. She wasn't even sick.

We had known she was dying for over eight months. The cancer was in her lung. Bud had not even gone to visit her in the hospital. He claimed she was "away somewhere."

"She's having an affair," he insisted.

The grave, I'm afraid, meant nothing to Bud. It was just another of Katie's wild excuses to ignore his needs.

Here's what happened — and the only reason I'm telling you this is that I want to put it on record. I want someone to know. The way some lives work out, you'd think the King of Clichés came in to write them. Bud's life was like that: shabby; squalid, like Katie's death.

I am an actor — and because I am an actor, I have had — for almost forty years — contact with well-written lives. When an actor throws up his hands and cannot manage to play a role, his response is always going to be: *I can't do this because I don't believe it.*

Katie's death and the nominal "end" of my brother's life were like that. No one in their right mind could make them believable. The facts and the images are too banal for words. Embarrassing.

The worst of Katie's condition came when she needed oxygen and nursing care at home. All this was seen as an inconvenience of monumental proportions from Bud's point of view.

A nurse, whose name was Sandra Ossington, came to give Katie baths and to oversee the regimen of pills and the supply of oxygen. Sometimes, when very drunk, Bud wouldn't let Ms Ossington come in. He'd lock the door and shout at her: *go away!* Katie then had to barricade herself in her room for fear that Bud would come in with a cigarette when she had the oxygen turned on.

The canisters of oxygen would be delivered by a man on schedule. He would always take away the expended tank and replace it with the new. He did this by rote according to a list that was given to him every day. He could hardly afford the time to say *hello*, let alone the time to argue about his right to enter the house. Once, when Katie was desperate to breathe and the oxygen man arrived, she had to phone the police in order to have Bud restrained. In the meantime, the oxygen man was forced to continue on his rounds because his other clients' needs were just the same as Katie's: a matter of life and death.

After that incident, Katie left Bud and their rented house in Scarborough and came down into Forest Hill, where she stayed with her cousin Jean. Jean gave me a call and said: "we're going to have to take Katie in. She can't go home again."

So a system was devised whereby — to all intents and purposes — Katie played the fugitive, "hiding out" first with Jean and then with me and then with a friend from work whose name was Gloria.

Gloria hated Bud with alarming vehemence. She once went up and threatened to burn the house down if Bud didn't let her in to collect Katie's things. This was about six weeks before Katie died and I guess we were all on Gloria's side and cheered her on. That's when Bud decided his wife was having an affair. He even went so far as to say she was having the affair with Gloria. Gloria had to be restrained.

The image of Bud and Gloria shouting on the lawn is funny, I suppose. Or it would be — perhaps — if Katie hadn't been so badly off. Shortly thereafter, she went into Sunnybrook Hospital — called every day for Bud — never heard from him and died.

The last time I saw Katie myself before she went into Sunnybrook, she was standing off in the distance, unaware that I was there. This was at the White Rose Nursery out in Unionville, and I had gone to buy a fern or something. Katie always made a garden wherever she lived with Bud and she left behind about a dozen perfect flower beds filled with her need for sanity and peace. I guess that day in

Unionville she was making up for the fact she would never walk in a garden again. I saw the look of loss on her face and turned around and walked away. It was unbearable: the loneliness.

I've already said Bud wouldn't come to the lying-in. A mass of others came instead — and that was the one good moment in all of this, the moment when all the twenty years of tension fell away and all the friends came through the door of the funeral home to say goodbye. I'm glad I was there; it gave me back — in that moment — something tangible of hope.

The burial itself was sad. Bud stood shaking when he saw the coffin. That was the moment when it dawned on him: *Katie is dead and gone forever.* He sat down hard on the ground beside the grave and his mouth fell open when he tried to speak. I had to go and lift him up and lead him away because, when he started to move, he seemed to want to follow her.

Later, though — and who am I to say it was not a blessing? — Bud denied being present at the funeral. How could he have been present when it hadn't even happened?

The phone rang twice every day all summer after that — (Katie died in May). By the fall, Bud was calling up at four o'clock in the morning, begging me to say he wasn't going to die. Somehow, if someone said it, he seemed to be genuinely reassured. Afterwards, he would natter on about what meals he'd eaten, where he'd been and who he'd seen.

The food was all-important. He could talk for hours about it.

I don't know why I believed him — but, like a fool, I did. He was so convincing, the way he told about the cuts of meat he would buy at Loblaws and the way he had cooked the potatoes — and all the herbs he used when making up the salad. His meals were almost poems to listen to. He loved the names of all the vegetables: *broccoli, spinach, zucchini* and he'd tell me which wines he'd drunk and he complained of all the prices.

He also had a lot to say about the friends who had begun to return his calls — the houses he had been in and the restaurants downtown. His social life was picking up. He was a normal human being again.

That was the trigger, of course: the word *again*. Bud had never been a normal human being in all his adult life.

Just about then it was getting on for a year since Katie's death and it was nearly May, Bud's birthday month. The phone calls — now that I wanted them — stopped. I had thought, since he was going about in the world, I would take him out for supper. Bud and I had not been out together for a century.

I waited for a week before I began the process in reverse. I called him three and four times a day. He didn't answer.

I telephoned our mother.

I didn't want to alarm her. I tried to say it diffidently, laughing because he was leaving me alone for a change. But I was interested...had she heard from Bud?

No.

Her story was more or less the same as mine. She had been receiving the same reports: the food — the outings —

the friends. Now, for several days, there had been nothing.

"I'll go around and see what's happening," I told her. Finally, I was worried. Very.

Looking at the house, I knew there was something wrong. Some of the lights were on. The car was parked in the driveway. I turned around and went away. I couldn't bear the thought of finding him dead.

I got the police and they had to break down the door. I waited on the lawn while they called for an ambulance. Someone barely alive had been found inside the house: almost a skeleton.

The corridor was dark and filled with beds and between the beds a stream of people, most of them hospital staff, was flowing — it seemed — almost entirely in my direction. All of them were blank-eyed; busy. At the nursing station they had said that I would find my brother down this corridor somewhere near the end.

I was walking towards a patch of vivid sunlight streaming through a window — almost blinding because the corridor was like a cave. There were three or four wheelchairs parked with their backs to me — facing this window — draped with rugs and ostensibly containing passengers, although I could see no evidence of this. There weren't any legs or arms or the backs of any heads that I could see.

"I'm looking for my brother, Thomas Cable," I said to an orderly who had just been arranging the wheelchairs in the sunlight.

The orderly said, without inflection: "you're standing

164

right beside him. That's his chair you have your hand on."

I walked around and stood in front of Bud.

Before me sat a man of almost eighty − whose mouth was hanging open and whose hands lay helpless in his lap − whose legs were so weak and thin they lay against each other, caved in against the side of the chair. His neck would barely support his head and his chin was resting on his collar-bone. I knelt before this man and called him *Bud* and told him who I was.

He stirred − uneasy − and he tried to move his hands and lift his chin, but he couldn't. I did that for him.

Looking back at me, he struggled desperately to understand why I should know his name and why he should think I seemed to be someone he knew. But he could not manage this. I was a stranger to him.

"How old is he?" the orderly asked.

"He's fifty-six," I said.

The orderly grunted.

"He can't have eaten in almost a month," he said.

I smiled. I thought of all the meals that Bud had described − and all the restaurants and all the wine.

"He's been on a liquid diet," I said   as lightly as I could

The doctor − a knowledgeable, pleasant little man whose sunny disposition somewhat threw me until I got to know him better − told me that Bud was suffering from something called Korsakov's syndrome. In short, this means that a part of Bud's brain has been destroyed and that, while he might live for many years, he will never recover the whole of his past and never quite understand who he is. He will know his name and he will recognize, from time to time, some specific incident from his life. Otherwise, Bud is locked — and will remain so — in a time zone from which he cannot escape.

He knows me, now, but every time I visit, he behaves as if we were at home and children and he wants to know where I have been.

You look so old, he will say to me. *Why have you grown so much older than me?*

I do not respond to this. I simply acknowledge that I am aberrant and Bud accepts this fact as being sufficient explanation. Sometimes, he smiles. I guess he knows what aberrant means.

He wants to see our parents and I have to tell him — every visit — that our mother has been ill and cannot come, just now, to see him. And then I have to tell him — every visit — that our father is dead and Bud is not surprised, but merely curious that his father could die and Bud not know it. *He must have died while I was away*, he will say. And I say nothing.

Every visit, too, he asks me where he is and who *these people* are. I do not tell him he is in a clinic for the aged because this would distress him. He does not know that he will not be leaving. He recognizes it must be some kind of rest home because the nurses and the doctors come and go and, time to time, somebody dies and is taken away.

On one occasion he asks me; "am I mad?"

I tell him: "no. You have been ill and we don't know why."

"Will you come and see me?"

"Yes."

"I get very lonely here," he says. "But the food is good."

I smile.

He looks at me, crooked — Bud grown old, a very old

166

man — and he says: "I'm missing someone, Neil. And I don't know who it is."

I hold his hand. He is greatly distressed and he rides along the edge of what remains of memory — peering out into the dark and trying desperately to see who might be there and to remember.

"Never mind," I tell him. "Honestly; no one is missing. Everything's fine."

"Where has our father gone?" he says.

I tell him. And I leave.

Every so often — maybe fifteen times a year — we will hold this meeting until he dies.

The day the police broke down the door and found him, I went with him to the hospital and gave him up in all his blankets and sheets to the doctors and the nurses in the Emergency Ward. Being told there was nothing to be done but wait and see if he would survive, I decided to return and await the news in Bud and Katie's rented house.

When I got there, it was nearing four o'clock in the afternoon and Katie's black cat was sitting on the porch. His name was Bubastis and we had met before.

Bubastis, however, would not come into the house. He seemed confused and wary and he kept his distance. I supposed he must be after food — he looked so thin — and I guessed that Bud had given up feeding him. Perhaps he had been coming for days to sit on the porch in the hopes that Bud would open the door and put down his meal.

I wished then, fervently, that we could talk to animals. How else could I explain to this beast that Katie was dead and Bud was probably going to die — as I thought that afternoon — and I would be more than happy to take Bubastis back with me to my house....

But no. He would have to wonder, perhaps forever, where all his people had gone and why they had deserted him. He went away and sat in the yard and I went into the house.

I opened a can of cat food and put the whole thing, dumped on a plate, onto the porch and called him.

"Bubastis!"

He did not come while I was standing there, but he must have come in the next half-hour because when I returned to the porch both the cat and all the food had disappeared.

Inside the house I found a wilderness of bottles and glasses and a maze of unmade beds, undusted furniture and piled-up cardboard boxes.

I looked and saw where Bud had been found. He had been lying — dressed in slacks and shirt, bare-footed, facing Katie's bed — in the hallway between their rooms. His own dark bedroom was behind him and the sheets on his bed were grey with age. On Katie's pillow, a note was pinned with a safety-pin and the note was in Katie's hand and it said: *Bud — Honey — I am going now and I won't be back. I've left a hundred dollars hidden in the hall closet. Look in the usual place and it will be there. I'm scared, right now, and I guess the thing is, soon I'm going to die. I wish you would come and see me. I will always love you, honey. Thank you for everything. Katie.*

She could only have written this before she made her escape to her cousin Jean, and that had been over a year ago. In all that time, the note had remained on Katie's pillow — and her bed exactly as she left it: the coverlet thrown back — the nightdress abandoned — her glass of water spilled and fallen to the floor.

In the kitchen, the smell was that of an abattoir; all the raw meat was so far gone it was alive with maggots. Bags of potatoes were sprouting in the corner. The sink was filled with dishes and the only evidence of food Bud might have truly eaten was a brace of opened and empty cans of Habitant pea soup. Four or five wide, flat boxes indicated that pizza had been delivered — but none of it had been removed and all of it was now a rotted sequence of red-and-yellow wheels.

Bud must have had some temper tantrums. Several dishes were broken — cigarettes and ash had been scattered over the floor and a case of beer appeared to have been struck a dozen blows by a hammer.

The living-room, which had once been charming under Katie's hand, was the wilderness already described of opened and unopened liquor bottles and glasses. Ashtrays were sprouting mould. A mouse had drowned in a vase of flowers. The telephone sat beside Bud's chair — unanswered all those days — and the television set was playing one of the soaps. I turned it off.

There by the telephone, neatly printed in Bud's distinctive hand, were Teddy Hartley's telephone number, the date — April 2 — and Dorothy Parker's poem.

I hoped, in that moment, for everyone's sake — especially his own — that Bud would die. That was the option he had chosen. And I had screwed it up by sending in the police.

I got down off the porch where the cat had finished the food and I went along the driveway past the garbage cans and into the large backyard.

169

Here, I was confronted by what I can only call the last bloody straw.

Katie's beloved flower beds had all spilled out across the uncut lawn – and the only thing in bloom was a mile-and-a-half wide carpet of forget-me-nots.

Forget-me-nots.

I ask you!

And sitting right in the middle, black as the ace of spades, was the cat, Bubastis – staring at me – asking me: *why?*

On either side of the fireplace, back in the living-room, all of Bud's books had been lined up in rows on shelves. When I thought of them, I thought how Bud had loved them and been nourished by them all those years and years ago when he was young and had wanted to be a writer. That was when he'd progressed from Erle Stanley Gardner to Joseph Conrad, Evelyn Waugh and F. Scott Fitzgerald. And I thought how unjust it was that all the mad and alcoholic heroes of whom these men had written should pass along through time forever, with their tragedies perfectly formed around their names and their lives set out in lucid prose with all the points well made and all the meanings clear. And I thought if only some great, compassionate novelist had been assigned to flesh out Bud and Katie's tragedy, they might have had a better ending to their lives than this.

Really, I thought, as I stood that afternoon and stared at Bubastis down among the forget-me-nots – *real life writes real bad. It should take lessons from the masters.*

ALMEYER'S
MOTHER

There was a time when Almeyer's mother chose not to visit him. The choice did not appear to be an arbitrary one — nor did it seem a calculated gesture of reproach. Mrs Almeyer had always maintained a certain distance from those who should have been closest to her: husband, brother and son. Uncle Charlie Walker, for instance, had not seen his sister in over fourteen years.

"I can't talk, Charlie," she would say on the phone. "Not today."

After a dozen or so rebuffs of this kind, Charlie Walker got the picture and gave up calling. Still, it made him sad, because he was otherwise alone and had a need for family ties.

As for Almeyer himself, he assumed his mother's refusal to visit had to do with his father's illness. Mister Almeyer suffered from Parkinson's disease and he needed endless attention. Even when he was hospitalized, Mrs Almeyer did not abandon him; her regimen of journeys to his bedside — twice a day on the bus — was followed seven days a week for five intolerable years.

Mornings, she would take her husband sandwiches made on homemade bread and they would sit in the rotunda, far apart from others, together in the shadows. Mister Almeyer had always been a man of impeccable taste and habit, so Mrs Almeyer carried a large, flat box of Kleenex tissues in her canvas carry-all and she would lean towards her husband, helping the food to reach its destination, dabbing at his mouth and wiping away the crumbs and saliva. During this, she would calm his waving arms by grasping his wrists and forcing them into his lap. Mister Almeyer, when he was not in bed, was a captive in a wheelchair and after they had eaten their sandwiches Mrs Almeyer would take him out for a "walk" in the grounds. She once showed Olive Marks, her maid, the muscles she had developed pushing the chair, and she gave up wearing short sleeved dresses because she thought the muscles unbecoming.

Evenings, after she had dined at home and spent the news hour seated alone in front of the television set, Mrs Almeyer would don her overcoat and set out once again for Sunnybrook Hospital. There she stayed with her husband for another hour and a half. Most times, she brought her needlework.

Wielding her threads with an artist's precision, never once losing her rhythm, Mrs Almeyer listened while her husband repeated for the hundredth time the story of his life. She let him do this without recrimination – not really minding she had heard it all before. Her ear was keen as her eye was sharp, and she was always listening for some new detail, something she hoped might provide the explanation of her discontent.

By the time Mister Almeyer had died, however, the explanation of her discontent had still not been forthcoming. Once, she received what she thought might be a hint of it. This was when he told her that, despite her long suspicions, he had never been unfaithful to her.

The only trouble was that Mrs Almeyer had no memory of having expected her husband's fidelity in the first place. Still, she never said so. What would the point have been, this late in the game, to call his bluff? She knew he was lying. What he was doing was seeking her approbation, not her forgiveness.

Mrs Almeyer nodded then and said *I believe you, Frank.* Better to pretend that nothing was amiss, now that everything was over.

Later, when he died, she hoped he would not be made to pay in excess for his earthly transgressions. Surely the Parkinson's had been enough.

Almeyer and his mother did, of course, see one another from time to time. Beside the formalities of Christmas dinners and birthday celebrations, they took occasional lunches together in the members' lounge of the Royal Ontario Museum.

Mrs Almeyer believed the flag of family unity had to be waved periodically in other people's faces; otherwise, the world was bound to talk. But there was no point waving the flag on Yonge Street; no point wasting your energies on chance encounters with those whose opinions gave you place and saved your face. Venue was everything in social matters, and the ROM, especially on Fridays, was the perfect place to create the image of a family's solidarity.

Sometimes — though less and less as the years went by — Almeyer's wife, Julie Fielding, would be present at these lunches. Julie made no pretence of enjoying her encounters with her husband's mother. She knew precisely what Edith Almeyer was up to. The wielding of the blades had begun almost as soon as Julie was married: the light, apparently offhand references to the fashion houses where she might just find that dress she *so obviously wanted*.... The asides, with a smile, about the mistakes Mrs Almeyer herself had made when she was young: *I remember rushing out to have my hair cut off like yours. But you'll find, soon enough, it will grow back in....*

Mrs Almeyer always listened with what Julie called *polite impatience* to anything her son had to say about his teaching job. She had never much cared for his eager approach to education; the subject offended her sense of dignity. Almeyer's discipline was English and his speciality was drama. This brought him dangerously close to public displays of emotion. Worse, it offered him the chance to encourage displays of emotion by others.

As for Julie, Mrs Almeyer openly resented the fact her daughter-in-law had chosen a profession that kept her so many hours away from home. When Almeyer had told his mother Julie was a social worker, she had sighed and said: *oh, Peter, she will always be dealing with someone else's problems; never with her own. And never yours.* Mrs Almeyer rightly predicted Julie would decline to raise a family.

Still, Mrs Almeyer never went so far as to press these

points in public. Listening to her son, she would allow her expression to register just the right degree of uncritical interest. The focus of her real attentions might more likely be the composition of a neighbour's luncheon party or the reflection, faraway across the room, of herself, her boy and his wife as they sat above their chicken salads, safe amidst the worthy patrons of Chinese art and Ira Berg. Mrs Almeyer yearned to drift there, floating in a sea of marble table tops forever. *This is us*, the picture informed her, *sitting where we belong.*

Almeyer's farm was south of Collins Corners, north of Whitby. The house had been built in 1839 by a man named Eli Steele. Steele descendants lived there up until 1972. Then, for five years, the house and the barns stood empty. When Almeyer took up his duties at the local high school in 1977, he and Julie had been married for a year. Seeing the condition the Steele house was in, they knew they might be able to afford it. Now, they had been there over ten years and all the fallen ceilings and the peeling walls had been repaired and the dense Victorian gardens had been reclaimed and the high stone wall that stood between the house and the road had been repointed.

The land was rented out to a man whose breeding stock could use the pasture and the barns were filled with hay that smelled of sweet grass. Almeyer bought an English setter and called him George, and they took long walks together down in the woods. Julie — who was an easy mark — was given three stray cats by one of her welfare cases, and their progeny now had multiplied to twenty. Everywhere you looked, it seemed, on a summer's day, a cat was looking back at you.

Once or twice in every season, Almeyer's parents would arrive and his father would honk the Buick's horn and George would bark and all the cats would run and hide. Almeyer and Julie would go out laughing and waving and bring in the picnic hampers, the rugs, the canvas bags and the one big suitcase — and Mister and Mrs Almeyer would be ensconced upstairs in the room beside the bathroom. Mister Almeyer — every single visit — pointing at the big brass bed, would say: *my grandmother had a woven quilt like that. She called it "Lee's Surrender."*

Mrs Almeyer had an allergy to cats and the door to the bedroom had to be closed against their intrusion every night. George would sit outside the door and whine for hours and throw his paws against the handle, rattling it and trying to get inside. He had taken, for whatever reason, a liking to Mister Almeyer and sometime after twelve o'clock every night, Almeyer would hear his father padding to the bedroom door and opening it. *In you come, Georgie! Don't wake Edith*, his father would say, and George would click across the boards and leap up right onto Mrs Almeyer's feet.

This midnight ritual, with all its attendant curses, whisperings and struggles for bed supremacy, was the one clear picture Almeyer had of his parents' final years together. Mister Almeyer always won the day by convincing his wife that George would act as a guarantee against the intrusion of Julie's cats. Silence would ensue. And sleep.

Mister Almeyer treated Julie much as if his son had won her in a contest. *Look what our boy's brought home*, he would say as he put his arm too far around her shoulder and gave the underside of her breast a flick with his fingers. Mrs Almeyer would go on sewing and pay no attention. Her husband had played this game with his nieces until their father had put a stop to it one Sunday afternoon. Julie, for her part, tolerated his touch because she wanted to see what effect the spectacle would have on Mrs Almeyer. Maybe, if she pushed it far enough, she would drive them from the house and they would not return. It never came to this, however. Time intervened and Julie herself departed.

During their visits, Mrs Almeyer tended to disappear in the late afternoons and did not return until the cocktail hour. She would come in from the gardens, carrying either a branch of coloured leaves or a rough bouquet of grasses, weeds and wild flowers. She would place these trophies in one of Almeyer's collection of blue china vases or a pressed-glass tumbler and these, in turn, she would disperse about the lower rooms of the house — searching for the very place to set each one down as if she was afraid of being still.

Why don't you sit, for heaven's sake, her husband would say, *and give us all a rest.*

Almeyer's mother, distracted and distant — not yet fully recovered from her afternoon outside — would say *I will. I will, Frank. Yes…* and perhaps in twenty minutes she would stop and find a chair. Her drink was always the same: a double scotch with one piece of ice. She drank this very slowly, waiting for the ice to melt before she finished.

In the evenings after dinner, Mister Almeyer wanted to sing. Almeyer's old and out-of-tune piano took a mighty beating beneath his father's lurching hands: still, it provided rousing renditions of "Lili Marlene" and "Waltzing Matilda." This way the days would end, and whenever Mister and Mrs Almeyer left, the house retained the echoes of their bickerings and songs. Two or three days later, Almeyer would move through the lower rooms and gather up the blue china vases and the pressed-glass tumblers filled with leaves and grass and drooping flowers and, passing the fireplace, he would throw these remnants of his mother's bouquets amongst the charred remains of cereal boxes, paper bags and the emptied containers of dog and cat chow that had served as the kindling for Mister Almeyer's unsuccessful fires.

Very often, walking with George in the garden, Almeyer would discover an abandoned crystal goblet, a dew-stained paperback book or a wad of Kleenex left behind from his mother's visits. She seemed to have a predilection for the yard, which gave a view, one way, of the orchard gently sloping down towards the river. Looking the other way, east, the side yard gave a view of the screened-in porch that ran across the front of the house. Mrs Almeyer evidently sat out there in the yard on the swing suspended from one of the maple trees, because Almeyer found the detritus of her presence mostly in the swing's vicinity. The goblets might enclose an amber drowning pool of undrunk whisky showing the corpses of ants and bees. One of the wads of Kleenex contained the butt of a cigarette. The books were less explicit in their declarations of his mother's state of mind: what could you learn from a Martha Grimes mystery? Once, he thought he might have tracked her down when he found a ruined copy of John Cheever's stories and he thought of all the unhappy people crowded in between its covers. Here, as if to place herself amongst the others, his mother had written her name in the flyleaf: *E.M. Almeyer.*

Of course, when Mister Almeyer's Parkinson's disease overtook his abilities altogether, the visits came to an end. This way life remained until about the sixth week after his death, when the telephone rang one evening and Almeyer's mother said from her house in Toronto: *I'm coming out.*

The Almeyer car, while Mister Almeyer lived, had always been a Buick and had always been maroon. Now that he was dead, Mrs Almeyer favoured something smaller and something more in line with the range of colours in which she dressed. A week before she phoned her son to warn him of her arrival, she had gone up Yonge Street in a taxi one day and looked in all the windows of the major dealers. Nothing really pleased her until they got to Richmond Hill. Here, she suddenly told the driver to stop because she had seen a flash of royal blue beyond an expansive sheet of glass.

The car turned out to be a *New Yorker* two-door sedan and she bought it on the spot. She had never done anything so extravagant in all her life and when she got back home and told Olive Marks what she had done, she was sure that, any moment, Mister Almeyer would come around the corner from his bedroom and ask her what the hell she thought she was doing.

Olive Marks reached up over the sink and brought down a bottle of the whisky kept for company. (Mrs Almeyer drank a cheaper brand of whisky when she was alone.) Then she poured two neat drinks and handed one across to Mrs Almeyer.

"Here's to that motor trip you always wanted," she said.

Mrs Almeyer went and sat in the living-room. She did not turn on the lights. Tippling her whisky, she gazed out the windows across the lawn and into the street.

I've bought a blue sedan, she thought. And then she wondered what to do with the rest of her life. Maybe she would drive away and not come back.

Almeyer had lived alone for the last two years before his father died. Julie Fielding had developed a battery of seniors in her department who thought she had "more potential than was useful" in Collins Corners. At their behest, she had returned to improve her status at the University of Toronto. She took up living there with a girl whose name was Sandra Givens. Sandra was somewhat younger than Julie, and her coterie of friends and acquaintances opened doors to ways of life that Julie had not before considered. Her manner changed — and the style of her aggression. Almeyer, at first, had been happy to run a few carloads of her books and winter clothes to Toronto, but when she telephoned one day and told him to bring her favourite cat, he refused.

"Why are you refusing me?" she asked.

"Because the cat is happy where it is," said Almeyer. Then he hung up.

Next day, he called the telephone company and had them change his number. He never heard from Julie Fielding again. Someone told him they had seen her with a man called Benson. That was all he knew of her, now.

His mother arrived on an afternoon in March. It was a Saturday. Almeyer had heard a crow that morning and he was excited. Hearing the first crow meant you had survived the winter.

He took his mother up to the room she had always shared with his father and showed her the improvements he had made in the bathroom. George walked everywhere they went and Mrs Almeyer reached down and petted him before she took her gloves off.

All that afternoon, he heard his mother roaming about the upper reaches of the house. He wondered if he ought to go up and see what might be troubling her. Maybe she needed something she could not find. He was on the point of starting up the stairs when he heard the door to her bedroom click and he thought: *she's going to have a rest.*

Round about four o'clock, he went outside to bring in firewood and, by the time he had filled the box, his mother had come downstairs and was waiting for him in the kitchen. "I've brought you something," she said. "It's something I want you to have. I think it belongs with you, but it's also something I have to explain."

Almeyer noticed an oblong package wrapped in brown paper sitting on the table. His mother had set it over on the far side, resting next to an already opened bottle of scotch. She held an empty glass in her hand, the glass he had left in the upstairs bathroom for her to put her toothbrush in. She was not by any means drunk but he could hear that she had started drinking. The sound of it was in her voice.

"Let's just sit out here in the kitchen," she said. "I haven't sat in a kitchen for years." She raised the bottle and filled her glass and then she passed the bottle to him. "Your health," she said, "and mine."

"Your health and mine," said Almeyer, getting himself a glass before he sat down. "What's in the package?"

Mrs Almeyer lighted a cigarette. Her first that month.

"I'm going to tell you something," she said. "I'm going to tell you something and then I don't know what I'm going to do. I may go home."

"Have I done something wrong?" said Almeyer.

"No," said his mother. "No. Just listen...."

Almeyer sat with George's head in his lap and listened. His mother's face was tilted down towards the table where her hands were wrapped around her glass and the cigarette smoke was rising into her swept-back hair. He thought he had never seen her quite so bereft of poise. She seemed immensely old and worn.

"Here," she said. "Undo the package. Look..."

Almeyer received the brown-paper parcel handed across the table. The minute he touched it, he knew it was a picture frame – perhaps with a picture inside. He pulled the paper away and threw it into an empty chair. Then he stared. Puzzled.

"Beautiful, isn't it," his mother said, her eyes on his.

"Yes. But I don't understand," said Almeyer. "Who are all these people?"

Resting in his hands, inside an imitation bamboo frame, there was a photograph. In the photograph, he recognized only his mother. She might have been as old as fifteen or as young as twelve and she was standing in a yard somewhere on a day in summer beside an older man who might have been – who must have been – her father. Both of them were smiling, each one looking at the other with almost alarming affection. Almeyer had never seen his grandfather before. His mother had said that pictures of him did not exist. Now, there he was and the sight of him – gazing down at his daughter – was so disturbing, Almeyer looked away. *Photographs that reveal such intimacy should not be taken,* he thought. *It isn't right.*

But he did not mention this. Instead, he ran his finger

along the faces of the others in the photograph: two young men and a woman leaning against a motor car. Almeyer thought he had never seen such beautiful boys, nor such a handsome woman.

"Is this your father?"

"Yes."

"Who are these other people, then?"

"Those are my brothers," his mother told him. "That was my mother."

Almeyer was astonished. The only brother he'd ever heard of was Uncle Charlie Walker, and though he could recall his grandmother — just — he could not reconcile the woman he remembered with the woman standing there before him in the photograph. The woman he remembered had lived in a house on St George Street and had been appallingly bad tempered and always dressed in black. She had died when Almeyer was four. "I don't understand," he said, his finger passing over the two young men. "Neither of these is Uncle Charlie."

"That's right," his mother said. "Uncle Charlie wasn't born yet. Even if he had been, he never could have stood there with us. My mother would not have allowed it."

"Why?"

"Because..." Mrs Almeyer smiled. She was nervous. "Uncle Charlie wasn't her son."

Almeyer did not know what to do or where to look. "How do you mean that?" he said. "Isn't he your brother?"

"Yes."

Almeyer waited.

Mrs Almeyer sipped her drink and let the glass go down towards the table, holding it just above the surface.

"I was thirteen," she said, "that summer. I had two brothers: there — the two you're looking at. One of them was older than me and the other one was younger. Harry was older. Tom was younger. Harry came of age the day that photograph was taken. Father had bought him that motorcar. Blue. It was a Chevrolet. this was in 1926. How long ago is that, now?"

"Sixty-two years."

"Sixty-two years. Yes. Well…The long and the short of it is, my father had forbidden Harry to go out driving after dark. But Harry was young — and he had these friends — and he had to show off his motor car. Did I say it was a Chevrolet?"

"Yes."

Mrs Almeyer continued: "I'm sure you can guess what happened. There was an accident. Harry was killed. No one knew at first who he was. Nor did they know who the other person was — the person who was killed beside him. Harry's motor car had been hit by a train and dragged for half a mile along the track. Someone, at last, found something of Harry's that gave his name and address and they came at seven in the morning, ringing the bell and pounding on the door. Agnes, our maid, went down and let them in and when my father was told what had happened he ran upstairs for Tom. And he called out *Tom! Tom! Wake up quick! We have to go and bring your brother home. He's dead*….And then there was a long, long silence and Tom could not be found because, of course, he had gone with Harry the night before. They both had disobeyed my father and they died."

Mrs Almeyer put more scotch in her glass and placed the bottle away from her over towards her son. Her cigarette had gone out and she tried to re-light it and could not and threw it down in the ashtry. Then she said:

"My parents did not recover. I was now their only child. My memory of it is that I used to hear them late at night —

186

beating at each other with their fists. I'm sure this can't be right — but it seems to be what I remember. My father begged my mother for another child. He wanted another child. *My boys! My boys!* he would say. *I want my boys!* It was awful. I have never, never seen such pain. We really thought that he would die of grief. But then..." Mrs Almeyer sighed. "Time passed. A week. A month. A year. And my father lived. We saw him less and less at home, and they saw him more and more at work. It seemed, for a while, to be all he did. He'd go downtown to the office — work until midnight — come home and fall into bed. My mother refused to sleep with him. Don't ask me why. That was her reaction. Perhaps she was afraid of having more children. All I do know is, she locked her door. Father took up another life. He was seen — he began to be seen in another part of town...."

Outside Almeyer's house, the sun had begun to set and all the stones in the wall were turning red and blue and the maple trees were mottled with orange. A breeze had risen and the swing beyond the porch was moving slowly back and forth and Almeyer's mother watched it — almost putting her fingers out to touch it.

"Friday, one week — it was April, now, and the rains had started and the birds were coming back — I heard my father talking for hours down in the library with my mother. Mother hardly spoke at all. My father went on and on and I wondered what it was. When my mother came upstairs to bed, she wept so long I thought she would never stop. Then, in the morning, my father said: *you're coming with me. Put on your overcoat, bring your umbrella and wear your rubber boots....*"

Mrs Almeyer smiled and lingered over the words a second time. "*Put on your overcoat. Bring your umbrella. Wear your rubber boots.* We walked and we walked. We walked in perfect silence, all the way into the other part of town where my father had been going alone for all those weeks and months after my mother locked her door."

Mrs Almeyer paused just long enough to select a Players cigarette from her pack, put it in her mouth and light it.

"We came to a charming little house that had a fence. It belonged to one of the men my father had befriended in the war. His name was Jerrold. Patterson Jerrold. And his house was set far back from the street beyond a lawn and trees. Just as we arrived, the sun came out and the air was warm and it smelled of rain and grass and daffodils. There were daffodils in Mister Jerrold's lawn. Then my father said *you wait here.* And he went away and I was left standing out in the side yard − just like your yard, there beyond the window. And there was a swing: a swing like yours − and the swing, the yard, the view of porches − it was all like that out there. All like that: exactly."

Almeyer was frightened. He wondered what his mother might be going to tell him.

"I sat," she said, "on the swing and I faced the house and I wondered why I was there. My father had not explained, except to say we were going to see Mister Jerrold who had been his friend in the war. I sat there half an hour and then − I heard a person moving on the porch behind the screens and the glass. *I can't,* I heard this person say, *please don't make me. I can't.* And I could see, beyond the reflections in the glass, two people moving − my father and another. And then, my father opened the door and he was smiling at me. *Smiling,*" said Mrs Almeyer. Then she said: "the porch, of course, was raised above the ground about a step − two steps − like yours. And just like yours, the door opened inwards so my father had to pull it towards him before he could come through. And he stepped down onto the grass, I remember, and he smiled and he said... *Edith, dear: there is someone here I want you to meet....*"

Mrs Almeyer placed her fingers in the air before her lips and she made a waving, brushing gesture, as if she was making room for someone to come and stand there between herself and her son: someone actual and real, of flesh.

"He put his hand back in towards the house and I saw another hand slip into his and this shadow figure moving forward into the light and... it was a girl. A girl with long, fine hair like mine and an oval face and shining eyes and she was beautiful. Beautiful. Lovely. And she stepped down onto the grass — wearing a pair of shiny new boots — and she wore an apron over her long, dark dress and my father said to me *Edith, this is Lily Jerrold*... I stood up, then, and I could see that Lily Jerrold was just my age — fourteen — fifteen — no more. And as she came towards me, proffered like a gift from my father, I suddenly saw that she was... She was pregnant."

Almeyer's mother looked at the swing in the yard beyond the window. Slowly, the breeze was dropping and it was still.

Then she said: "the long and short of it was, my father wanted to marry her. *The child would need a name*, he said. And I wondered, did he mean the child who stood before me, or the child she was carrying. Which?"

"And the child Lily Jerrold carried was Uncle Charlie Walker?"

"Yes. The child was Uncle Charlie Walker."

Almeyer and his mother sat for five or ten minutes drinking at the kitchen table. Mrs Almeyer kept her eye on the garden, watching it disappear into the growing darkness and watching the windows fading one by one across the length of the screened-in porch — and the wall with all its stones going out like a picture being erased.

"Why have you hidden this all this time?" said Almeyer. "Did you think I wouldn't understand?"

"You don't understand," his mother said. "Look at the photograph. Look at my father's eyes. You've always wondered why there were no pictures of him. I destroyed all the rest, but I kept this one because I had to be able to look at him. But I couldn't bear the way he looked at me...."

The clock ticked.

"Don't you see?" she said. "If it hadn't been for Lily Jerrold — what might have happened to me?"

Almeyer gave no answer.

Later that night, Almeyer went outside with George and looked at the moon.

His mother's new car was parked like a ghost in the courtyard. Uncles he had never known existed before hovered in the air above it. George went away in search of trees. Almeyer looked up past the car and saw his mother's light go out. He wondered if she had ever told her father how she had been afraid of him. He wondered if her father had ever been reconciled to that. And he wondered if Lily Jerrold had ever become her friend.

After a while, he called the dog and they went inside.

The next day was Sunday, but when Almeyer awoke, his mother and her car were gone.

I don't know where I'm going, she wrote in the note she

left on his kitchen table. *When I get there, I'll let you know.*

She signed this:

E.M. Almeyer,

Your mother.

Something in the signature informed him she would always be alone. There was nothing he could do.

STONES

We lived on the outskirts of Rosedale, over on the wrong side of Yonge Street. This was the impression we had, at any rate. Crossing the streetcar tracks put you in another world.

One September, my sister, Rita, asked a girl from Rosedale over to our house after school. Her name was Allison Pritchard and she lived on Cluny Drive. When my mother telephoned to see if Allison Pritchard could stay for supper, Mrs Pritchard said she didn't think it would be appropriate. That was the way they talked in Rosedale: very polite; oblique and cruel.

Over on our side — the west side — of Yonge Street, there

were merchants — and this, apparently, made the difference to those whose houses were in Rosedale. People of class were not meant to live in the midst of commerce.

Our house was on Gibson Avenue, a cul-de-sac with a park across the road. My bedroom window faced a hockey rink in winter and a football field in summer. Cy, my brother, was a star in either venue. I was not. My forte, then, was the tricycle.

Up at the corner, there was an antique store on one side and a variety shop on the other. In the variety shop, you could spend your allowance on penny candy, Eskimo pies and an orange drink I favoured then called *Stubby*. *Stubby* came in short, fat bottles and aside from everything else — the thick orange flavour and the ginger in the bubbles — there was something wonderfully satisfying in the fact that it took both hands to hold it up to your lips and tip it down your throat.

Turning up Yonge Street, beyond the antique store, you came to The Women's Bakery, Adam's Grocery, Oskar Schickel, the butcher and Max's Flowers. We were Max's Flowers. My mother and my father wore green aprons when they stood behind the counter or went back into the cold room where they made up wreaths for funerals, bouquets for weddings and corsages for dances at the King Edward Hotel. Colonel Matheson, retired, would come in every morning on his way downtown and pick out a boutonnière from the jar of carnations my mother kept on the counter near the register. Once, when I was four, I caused my parents untold embarrassment by pointing out that Colonel Matheson had a large red growth on the end of his nose. The "growth" was nothing of the sort, of course, but merely the result of Colonel Matheson's predilection for gin.

Of the pre-war years, my overall memory is one of perfect

winters, heavy with snow and the smell of coal-and wood-smoke mingling with the smell of bread and cookies rising from The Women's Bakery. The coal-smoke came from our furnaces and the wood-smoke — mostly birch and maple — came to us from the chimneys of Rosedale, where it seemed that every house must have a fireplace in every room.

Summers all smelled of grass being cut in the park and burning tar from the road crews endlessly patching the potholes in Yonge Street. The heat of these summers was heroic and the cause of many legends. Mister Schickel, the butcher, I recall once cooked an egg on the sidewalk out-side his store. My father, who was fond of Mister Schickel, made him a bet of roses it could not be done. I think Mister Schickel's part of the bet was pork chops trimmed of excess fat. When the egg began to sizzle, my father slapped his thigh and whistled and he sent my sister, Rita, in to get the flowers. Mister Schickel, however, was a graceful man and when he placed his winnings in the window of his butcher shop, he also placed a card that read: *Thanks to Max's Flowers one dozen roses.*

The Great Depression held us all in thrall, but its effects on those of us who were used to relative poverty — living on the west side of Yonge Street — were not so debilitating as they were on the far side in Rosedale. The people living there regarded money as something you had — as opposed to something you went out and got — and they were slower to adjust to what, for them, was the unique experience of deprivation.

I remember, too, that there always seemed to be a tramp at the door: itinerants asking if — for the price of a meal, or the meal itself — they could carry out the ashes, sweep the walks or pile the baskets and pails in which my father brought his flowers from the market and the greenhouse.

Our lives continued in this way until about the time I was five — in August of 1939. Everyone's life, I suppose, has its demarcation lines — its latitudes and longitudes passing through time. Some of these lines define events that everyone shares — others are confined to personal — even to secret lives. But the end of summer 1939 is a line drawn down through the memory of everyone who was then alive. We were all about to be pitched together into a melting pot of violence from which a few of us would emerge intact and the rest of us would perish.

My father joined the army even before the war had started. He went downtown one day and didn't come back till after suppertime. I noticed that he hadn't taken the truck but had ridden off on the streetcar. I asked my mother why he had worn his suit on a weekday and she replied *because today is special*. But that was all she said.

At the table, eating soufflé and salad, my brother, Cy — who was nine years old that summer — talked about the World's Fair in New York City and pictures he'd seen of the future in magazines. The Great World's Fair was a subject that had caught all our imaginations with its demonstrations of new appliances, aeroplanes and motor cars. Everything was "streamlined" in 1939; everything designed with swept-back lines as if we were all preparing to shoot off into space. Earlier that summer, the King and Queen of England had come to Canada, riding on a streamlined train whose blue-painted engine was sleek and slim as something in a silver glove. In fact, the King and Queen had arrived in Toronto just up Yonge Street from where we lived. We got permission from the Darrow family, who lived over Max's Flowers, to stand on the roof and watch the parade with its

Mounties in scarlet and its Black Watch Band and the King and Queen, all blue and white and smiling, sitting in an open Buick called a *McLaughlin — built*, according to Cy, *right here in Canada!* For one brief moment while all these symbols of who we were went marching past, the two communities — one on either side of Yonge Street — were united in a surge of cheering and applause. But after the King and Queen were gone, the ribbon of Yonge Street divided us again. It rained.

Now, Cy and Rita were arguing over the remnants in the soufflé dish. Cy held the classic belief that what was in the dish was his by virtue of his being the eldest child. He also held the classic belief that girls were meant to be second in everything. Rita, who was always hungry but never seemed to gain an ounce, held none of these beliefs and was capable of fighting Cy for hours on end when our parents weren't present. With Mother at the table, however, the argument was silenced by her announcement that the soufflé dish and all the delicious bits of cheese and egg that clung to its sides would be set aside for our father.

Then — or shortly thereafter — our father did indeed arrive, but he said he wasn't hungry and he wanted to be left alone with Mother.

In half an hour the children were called from the kitchen where we had been doing the dishes and scooping up the remains of the meal. I — the child my mother called *The Rabbit* — had been emptying the salad bowl, stuffing my mouth with lettuce, tomatoes and onion shards and nearly choking in the process. We all went into the sitting-room with food on our lips and tea towels in our hands: Father's three little Maxes — Cy and Rita and Ben. He looked at us then, as he always did, with a measure of pride he could never hide and a false composure that kept his lips from smiling, but not his eyes. I look back now on that moment with some alarm when I realize my father was only twenty-seven years old — an age I have long survived and doubled.

"Children, I have joined the army," he said — in his formal way, as if we were his customers. "I am going to be a soldier."

Our mother had been weeping before we entered the room, but she had dried her eyes because she never allowed us to witness her tears. Now, she was smiling and silent. After a moment, she left the room and went out through the kitchen into the garden where, in the twilight, she found her favourite place and sat in a deck-chair amidst the flowers.

Cy, for his part, crowed with delight and yelled with excitement. He wanted to know if the war would last until he was a man and could join our father at the front.

Father, I remember, told him the war had not yet begun and the reason for his own enlistment was precisely so that Cy and I could not be soldiers. "There will be no need for that," he said.

Cy was immensely disappointed. He begged our father to make the war go on till 1948, when he would be eighteen.

Our father only laughed at that.

"The war," he said, "will be over in 1940."

I went out then and found our mother in the garden.

"What will happen to us while he's away?" I asked.

"Nothing," she said. And then she said: "come here."

I went and leaned against her thigh and she put her arm around my shoulder and I could smell the roses somewhere behind us. It was getting dark.

"Look up there," she said. "The stars are coming out. Why don't you count them?"

This was her way of distracting me whenever my questions got out of hand. Either she told me to count the stars or go outside and dig for China. *There's a shovel in the shed*, she would tell me. *You get started and I will join you.* Just as if we would be in China and back by suppertime.

But that night in August, 1939, I wasn't prepared to bite. I didn't want to dig for China and I didn't want to count the stars. I'd dug for China so many times and had so many holes in the yard that I knew I would never arrive; it was much too far and, somehow, she was making a fool of me. As for the stars: "I counted them last night," I told her. "And the night before."

"Oh?" she said — and I felt her body tense, though she went on trying to inject a sense of ease when she spoke. "So tell me," she said. "How many are there?"

"Twelve," I said.

"Ah," she said. And sighed. "Just twelve. I thought there might be more than twelve."

"I mean twelve zillion," I said with great authority.

"Oh," she said. "I see. And you counted them all?"

"Unh-hunh."

For a moment she was quiet. And then she said: "what about that one there?"

One week later, the war began. But my father had already gone.

On the 14th of February, 1943, my father was returned. He came back home from the war. He did this on a Sunday and I recall the hush that fell upon our house, as indeed it seemed to have fallen over all the city. Only the sparrows out in the trees made sound.

We had gone downtown to the Exhibition Grounds to meet him. The journey on the streetcar took us over an hour, but Mother had splurged and hired a car and driver to take us all home. The car, I remember, embarrassed me. I was afraid some friend would see me being driven — sitting up behind a chauffeur.

A notice had come that told us the families of all returning soldiers would be permitted to witness their arrival. I suspect the building they used for this was the one now used to house the Royal Winter Fair and other equestrian events. I don't remember what it was called and I'm not inclined to inquire. It was enough that I was there that once — and once remains enough.

We sat in the bleachers, Cy and Rita and Mother and me, and there was a railing holding us back. There must have been over a thousand people waiting to catch a glimpse of someone they loved — all of them parents, children or wives of the men returning. I was eight years old that February — almost nine and feeling I would never get there. Time was like a field of clay and all the other children I knew appeared to have cleared it in a single bound while I was stuck in the mud and barely able to lift my feet. I hated being eight and dreaded being nine. I wanted to be ten — the only dignified age a child could be, it seemed to me. Cy, at ten, had found a kind of silence I admired to the point of worship. Rita, who in fact was ten that year and soon to be eleven, had also found a world of silence in which she kept herself secreted — often behind closed doors. Silence was a sign of valour.

The occasion was barely one for public rejoicing. The men who were coming home were mostly casualties whose wounds, we had been warned, could be distressing and whose spirit, we had equally been warned, had been damaged in long months of painful recuperation. Plainly, it was our job to lift their spirits and to deny the severity of their wounds. Above all else, they must not be allowed to feel they could not rejoin society at large. A man with no face must not be stared at.

Our father's wounds were greater by far than we had been told. There was not a mark on his body, but — far inside — he had been destroyed. His mind had been severely damaged and his spirit had been broken. No one had told me what this might have made of him. No one had said *he may never be kind again.* No one had said *he will never sleep again without the aid of alcohol.* No one had said *he will try to kill your mother.* No one had said *you will not be sure it's him when you see him.* Yet all these things were true.

I had never seen a military parade without a band. The effect was eerie and upsetting. Two or three officers came forward into the centre of the oval. Somebody started shouting commands and a sergeant-major, who could not yet be seen, was heard outside the building counting off the steps.

I wanted drums. I wanted bugles. Surely this ghostly, implacable sound of marching feet in the deadening sand was just a prelude to everyone's standing up and cheering and the music blaring forth. But, no. We all stood up, it is true, the minute the first of the columns rounded the wooden corner of the bleachers and came into sight. But no one uttered a sound. One or two people threw their hands up over their mouths — as if to stifle cries — but most of us simply stood there — staring in disbelief.

Nurses came with some of the men, supporting them. Everyone was pale in the awful light — and the colours of their wounds and bruises were garish and quite unreal. There was a predominance of yellow flesh and dark maroon scars and of purple welts and blackened scabs. Some men wore bandages — some wore casts and slings. Others used canes and crutches to support themselves. A few had been the victims of fire, and these wore tight, blue skull-caps and collarless shirts and their faces and other areas of uncovered skin were bright with shining ointments and dressings.

It took a very great while for all these men and women — perhaps as many as two hundred of them — to arrive inside the building and make their way into the oval. They were being lined up in order of columns — several long lines, and each line punctuated here and there with attendant nurses. The voices of the sergeant-major and of the adjutant who was taking the parade were swallowed up in the dead acoustics, and — far above us — pigeons and sparrows moved among the girders and beams that supported the roof. I still had not seen Father.

At last, because my panic was spreading out of control, I tugged my mother's elbow and whispered that I couldn't see him. Had there been a mistake and he wasn't coming at all?

"No," she told me — looking down at me sideways and turning my head with her ungloved fingers. "There he is, there," she said. "But don't say anything, yet. He may not know we're here."

My father's figure could only be told because of his remarkable height. He was six feet four and had always been, to me, a giant. But now his height seemed barely greater than the height of half a dozen other men who were gathered out in the sand. His head was bowed, though once or twice he lifted his chin when he heard the commands. His shoulders, no longer squared, were rounded forward and dipping towards his centre. His neck was so thin I thought that someone or something must have cut over half of it away. I studied him solemnly and then looked up at my mother.

She had closed her eyes against him because she could not bear to look.

Later on that night, when everyone had gone to bed but none of us had gone to sleep, I said to Cy: "what is it?"

"What?"

"That's happened to Dad...."

Cy didn't answer for a moment and then he said: "Dieppe."

I didn't understand. I thought it was a new disease.

We were told the next day not to mention at school that our father had come back home. Nothing was said about why it must be kept a secret. That was a bitter disappointment. Other children whose fathers had returned from overseas were always the centre of attention. Teachers, beaming smiles and patting heads, would congratulate them just as if they had won a prize. Classmates pestered them with questions: *what does he look like? Have you seen his wounds? How many Germans did he kill?* But we had none of this. All we got was: *what did you do on the weekend?*

Nothing.

All day Monday, Father remained upstairs. Our parents' bedroom was on the second floor directly over the sitting-room. Also, directly underneath the bedroom occupied by Cy and me. We had heard our mother's voice long into the night, apparently soothing him, telling him over and over again that everything was going to be all right.

We could not make out her words, but the tone of her voice was familiar. Over time, she had sat with each of us, deploying her comforts in all the same cadences and phrases, assuring us that pains and aches and sicknesses would pass.

Because we could not afford to lose the sale of even one flower, neither the single rose bought once a week by Edna Holmes to cheer her ailing sister, nor the daily boutonnière of Colonel Matheson — our mother had persuaded Mrs Adams, the grocer's wife, to tend the store while she "nipped home" once every hour to see to Father's needs. It was only later that we children realized what those needs entailed. He was drinking more or less constantly in every waking hour, and our mother's purpose was first to tempt him with food — which he refused — and then to make certain that his matches and cigarettes did not set fire to the house.

On the Wednesday, Father emerged from his shell around two o'clock in the afternoon. We were all at school, of course, and I have only the account of what follows from my mother. When she returned at two, Mother found that Father had come down into the hallway, fully dressed in civilian clothes. He had already donned his greatcoat when she arrived. She told me that, at first, he had seemed to be remarkably sober. He told her he wanted to go outside and walk in the street. He wanted to go and see the store, he said.

"But you can't wear your greatcoat, David," she told him.

"Why?"

"Because you're in civilian dress. You know that's not allowed. A man was arrested just last week."

"I wasn't here last week," said my father.

"Nevertheless," my mother told him, "this man was arrested because it is not allowed."

"But I'm a soldier!" my father yelled.

My mother had to play this scene with all the care and cunning she could muster. The man who had been arrested had been a deserter. All that winter, desertions had been increasing and there had been demonstrations of overt disloyalty. People had shouted *down with the King!* and had booed the Union Jack. There were street gangs of youths who called themselves *Zombies* and they hung around the Masonic Temple on Yonge Street and the Palais Royale at Sunnyside. Some of these young men were in uniform, members of the Home Guard: reserves who had been promised, on joining up, they would not be sent overseas. They may have disapproved of the war, but they did not disapprove of fighting. They waited outside the dancehalls, excessively defensive of their manhood, challenging the servicemen who were dancing inside to *come out fighting and show us your guts!* Men had been killed in such encounters and the encounters had been increasing. The government was absolutely determined to stamp these incidents out before they spread across the country. These were the darkest hours of the war and morale, both in and out of the Forces, was at its lowest ebb. If my father had appeared on the street with his military greatcoat worn over his civilian clothes, it would have been assumed he was a *Zombie* or a deserter and he would have been arrested instantly. Our neighbours would have turned him in, no matter who he was. Our patriotism had come to that.

"I don't have a civilian overcoat," my father said. "And don't suggest that I put on my uniform, because I won't. My uniform stinks of sweat and I hate it."

"Well, you aren't going out like that," my mother said. "That's all there is to it. Why not come to the kitchen and I'll fix you a sandwich...."

"I don't want a goddamned sandwich," my father yelled at her. "I want to see the store!"

At this point, he tore off his greatcoat and flung it onto the stairs. And then, before my mother could prevent him, he was out the door and running down the steps.

My mother — dressed in her green shop apron and nothing but a scarf to warm her — raced out after him.

What would the neighbours think? What would the neighbours say? How could she possibly explain?

By the time she had reached the sidewalk, my father had almost reached the corner. But, when she got to Yonge Street, her fears were somewhat allayed. My father had not gone into Max's Flowers but was standing one door shy of it, staring into the butcher's window.

"What's going on here?" he said, as my mother came abreast of him.

Mother did not know what he meant.

"Where is Mister Schickel, Lily?" he asked her.

She had forgotten that, as well.

"Mister Schickel has left," she told him — trying to be calm — trying to steer my father wide of the butcher's window and in towards their own front stoop.

"Left?" my father shouted. "He's only just managed to pay off his mortgage! And who the hell is this imposter, Reilly?"

"Reilly?"

"Arthur Reilly the bloody butcher!" My father pointed at and read the sign that had replaced *Oskar Schickel, Butcher* in the window.

"Mister Reilly has been there most of the winter, David. Didn't I write and tell you that?" She knew very well she hadn't.

My father blinked at the meagre cuts of rationed meat displayed beyond the glass and said: "what happened to Oskar, Lily? Tell me."

And so, she had to tell him, like it or not.

Mister Schickel's name was disagreeable — stuck up there on Yonge Street across from Rosedale — and someone from Park Road had thrown a stone through the window.

There. It was said.

"But Oskar wasn't a German," my father whispered. "He was a Canadian."

"But his name was German, David."

My father put his fingers against the glass and did not appear to respond to what my mother had said.

At last, my mother pulled at his arm. "Why not come back home," she said. "You can come and see the shop tomorrow."

My father, while my mother watched him, concentrated very hard and moved his finger over the dusty glass of Oskar Schickel's store.

"What are you doing, David?"

"Nothing," said my father. "Setting things right, that's all."

Then he stepped back and said to her: "now — we'll go home."

What he had written was:

Oskar Schickel: Proprietor in absentia.

Mother said that Mrs Reilly rushed outside as soon as they had reached the corner and she washed the window clean.

209

This was the only remaining decent thing my father did until the day he died.

The rest was all a nightmare.

I had never seen Dieppe. I had seen its face in photographs. I had read all the books and heard all the stories. The battle, of which my father had been a victim, had taken place in August of 1942 — roughly six months before he was returned to us. Long since then, in my adult years, I have seen that battle, or seen its parts, through the medium of documentary film. It was only after Cy and Rita had vetted these films that I was able to watch. Till then, I had been afraid I would catch my father's image unawares — fearful that somehow our eyes would meet in that worst of moments. I couldn't bear the thought of seeing him destroyed. So, I had seen all this — the photographs, the books, the films — but I had never seen the town of Dieppe itself until that day in May of 1987 when I took my father's ashes there to scatter them.

Before I can begin this ending, I have to make it clear that the last thing I want to provoke is the sentimental image of a wind-blown stretch of rocky beach with a rainbow of ashes arching over the stones and blowing out to sea. If you want that image, let me tell you that had been the way it was when Cy, my brother, and Rita, my sister, and I went walking, wading into the ocean south of Lunenburg, Nova Scotia — where our mother had been born — to cast her ashes into the air above the Atlantic. Then there was almost music and we rejoiced because our mother had finally gained her freedom from a life that had become intolerable. But in Dieppe, when I shook my father's ashes out of their envelope, there was no rejoicing. None.

I felt, in fact, as if I had brought the body of an infidel into a holy place and laid it down amongst the true believers. Still, this was what my father had wanted — and how could I refuse him? Neither Cy nor Rita would do it for him. *Gone*, they had said. *Good riddance*.

And so it fell to me.

I was always the least informed. I was always the most inquisitive. During my childhood, nobody told me — aside from the single word *Dieppe* — what it was that had happened to my father. And yet, perhaps because I knew the least and because I was the youngest and seemed the most naïve and willing, it was more than often me he focused on.

His tirades would begin in silence — the silence we had been warned of when he first returned. He would sit at the head of the table, eating a piece of fish and drinking from a glass of beer. The beer was always dark in colour. Gold.

Our dining-room had a window facing west. Consequently, winter sunsets in particular got in his eyes.

Curtain, he would say at his plate — and jab his fork at me.

If I didn't understand because his mouth was full, my mother would reach my sleeve and pull it with her fingers. *The curtain, Ben*, she would say. *Your father's eyes*.

Yes, ma'am. Down I'd get and pull the curtain.

Then, no sooner would I be reseated than my father — still addressing his plate — would mumble *lights*. And I would rise and turn on the lights. Then, when I was back at last in my chair, he would look at me and say, without apparent rancour, *why don't you tell me to shove the goddamn curtain up my ass?*

You will understand my silence in response to this if you understand that — before he went away — the worst my

211

father had ever said in our presence had been *damn* and *hell*. The ultimate worst had been *Christ!* when he'd nearly sliced his finger off with a knife. Then, however, he hadn't known that anyone was listening. And so, when he started to talk this way — and perhaps especially at table — it paralyzed me.

Cy or Mother would sometimes attempt to intervene, but he always cut them off with something worse than he'd said to me. Then he would turn his attention back in my direction and continue. He urged me to refuse his order, then to upbraid him, finally to openly defy him — call him the worst of the words he could put in my mouth and hit him. Of course, I never did any of these things, but the urging, the cajoling and ultimately the begging never ceased.

One night, he came into the bedroom where I slept in the bunk-bed over Cy and he shouted at me *why don't you fight back?* Then he dragged my covers off and threw me onto the floor against the bureau. All this was done in the dark, and after my mother had driven me down in the truck to the Emergency Ward of Wellesley Hospital, the doctors told her that my collar-bone was broken. I heard my mother saying *yes, he fell out of bed*.

Everyone — even I — conspired to protect him. The trouble was, my father had no wish to protect himself. At least, it seemed that way until a fellow veteran of Dieppe turned up one day in the shop and my father turned on him with a pair of garden shears and tried to drive him back onto Yonge Street. Far from being afraid of my father, the other man took off his jacket and threw it in my father's face and all the while he stood there, the man was yelling at my father: *Coward! Coward! Yellow Bastard!*

Then, he turned around and walked away. The victor.

Thinking for sure the police would come, my mother drew the blind and closed the shop for the rest of the day.

But that was not the end of it. She gathered us together out on the porch and Cy was told to open a can of pork and beans and to make what our mother called a *passel of toast*. He and Rita and I were to eat this meal in the kitchen, after which Cy, who'd been handed a dollar bill my mother had lifted from the till, was to take us down to the Uptown Theatre where an Abbott and Costello film was playing. All these ordinary things we did. Nonetheless, we knew that our father had gone mad.

It was summer then and when the movie was over, I remember Cy and Rita and I stood on the street and the sidewalks gave off heat and the air around us smelled of peanuts and popcorn and Cy said: "I don't think it's safe to go home just yet." For almost an hour, we wandered on Yonge Street, debating what we should do and, at last, we decided we would test the waters by going and looking at the house and listening to see if there was any yelling.

Gibson Avenue only has about twenty houses, most of them semi-detached — and all of them facing south and the park. The porches and the stoops that night were filled with our neighbours drinking beer from coffee cups and fanning themselves with paper plates and folded bits of the *Daily Star*. They were drinking out of cups — you could smell the beer — because the law back then forbade the public consumption, under any circumstance, of alcohol. Whatever you can hide does not exist.

Passing, we watched our neighbours watching us — the Matlocks and the Wheelers and the Conrads and the Bolts

— and we knew they were thinking *there go the Max kids and David Max, their father, tried to kill a man today in his store with gardening shears....*

"Hello, Cy."

"Hello."

"Ben. Rita."

"Hi."

"Good-night…"

We went and stood together on the sidewalk out in front of our house.

Inside, everything seemed to be calm and normal. The lights were turned on in their usual distribution — most of them downstairs. The radio was playing. Someone was singing *Praise the Lord and Pass the Ammunition.*

Cy went up the steps and turned the handle. He was brave — but I'd always known that. Rita and I were told to wait on the porch.

Two minutes passed — or five — or ten — and finally Cy returned. He was very white and his voice was dry, but he wasn't shaking and all he said was: "you'd best come in. I'm calling the police."

Our father had tried to kill our mother with a hammer. She was lying on the sofa and her hands were broken because she had used them trying to fend off the blows.

Father had disappeared. The next day, he turned himself in because, as he told the doctors, he had come to his senses. He was kept for a year and a half — almost until the war was over — at the Asylum for the Insane on Queen Street. None of us children was allowed to visit him there — but our mother went to see him six months after he had been committed. She told me they sat in a long, grey room with bars on all the windows. My father wore a dressing gown and hadn't shaved. Mother said he couldn't look her

214

in the eyes. She told him that she forgave him for what he had done. But my father never forgave himself. My mother said she never saw his eyes again.

Two weeks after our father had tried to kill our mother, a brick was thrown through the window of Max's Flowers. On the brick, a single word was printed in yellow chalk.

Murderer.

Mother said: "there's no way around this, now. I'm going to have to explain."

That was how we discovered what had gone wrong with our father at Dieppe.

Our mother had known this all along, and I still have strong suspicions Cy had found it out and maybe Rita before our mother went through the formal procedure of sitting us down and telling us all together. Maybe they had thought I was just too young to understand. Maybe Cy and maybe Rita hadn't known. Maybe they had only guessed. At any rate, I had a very strong sense that I was the only one who received our mother's news in a state of shock.

Father had risen, since his enlistment in 1939, all the way up from an NCO to the rank of captain. Everyone had adored him in the army. He was what they called a natural leader. His men were particularly fond of him and they would, as the saying goes, have followed him anywhere. Then came Dieppe. All but a handful of those who went into battle there were Canadians. This was our Waterloo. Our Gettysburg.

There isn't a single history book you can read – there isn't a single man who was there who won't tell you –

215

there isn't a single scrap of evidence in any archive to suggest that the battle of Dieppe was anything but a total and appalling disaster. Most have called it a slaughter.

Dieppe is a port and market town on the coast of Normandy in northern France. In 1942, the British High Command had chosen it to be the object of a practice raid in preparation for the invasion of Europe. The Allies on every front were faltering, then. A gesture was needed, and even the smallest of victories would do.

And so, on the 19th of August, 1942, the raid on Dieppe had taken place — and the consequent carnage had cost the lives of over a thousand Canadians. Over two thousand were wounded or taken prisoner. Five thousand set out; just over one thousand came back.

My father never left his landing craft.

He was to have led his men ashore in the second wave of troops to follow the tanks — but, seeing the tanks immobilized, unable to move because the beaches were made of stone and the stones had jammed the tank tracks — and seeing the evident massacre of the first wave of troops whose attempt at storming the shore had been repulsed by machine-gun fire from the cliffs above the town — my father froze in his place and could not move. His men — it is all too apparent — did not know what to do. They had received no order to advance and yet, if they stayed, they were sitting ducks.

In the end, though a handful escaped by rushing forward into the water, the rest were blown to pieces when their landing craft was shelled. In the meantime, my father had recovered enough of his wits to crawl back over the end of the landing craft, strip off his uniform and swim out to sea where he was taken on board a British destroyer sitting offshore.

The destroyer, H.M.S. *Berkley*, was ultimately hit and everyone on board, including my father — no one knowing who he was — was transferred to another ship before the *Berkley* was scuttled where she sat. My father made it all the way back to England, where his burns and wounds were dressed and where he debated taking advantage of the chaos to disappear, hoping that, in the long run, he would be counted among the dead.

His problem was, his conscience had survived. He stayed and, as a consequence, he was confronted by survivors who knew his story. He was dishonourably discharged and sent home to us. Children don't understand such things. The only cowards they recognize are figures cut from comic books or seen on movie screens.

Fathers cannot be cowards.

It is impossible.

His torment and his grief were to lead my father all the way to the grave. He left our mother, in the long run, though she would not have wished him to do so and he lived out his days in little bars and back-street beer parlours, seeking whatever solace he could find with whores and derelicts whose stories might have matched his own. The phone would ring and we would dread it. Either it was him or news of him — either his drunken harangue or the name of his most recent jail.

He died in the Wellesley Hospital, the place where I was born — and when he was dying he asked to see his children. Cy and Rita "could not be reached," but I was found — where he'd always found me — sitting within yelling distance. Perhaps this sounds familiar to other children — of whatever age — whose parents, whether one of them or both of them, have made the mistake of losing faith too soon in their children's need to love.

I would have loved a stone.

If only he had known.

He sensed it, maybe, in the end. He told me he was sorry for everything — and meant it. He told me the names of all his men and he said he had walked with them all through hell, long since their deaths, to do them honour. He hoped they would understand him, now.

I said they might.

He asked if his ashes could be put with theirs.

Why not, I thought. *A stone among stones.*

The beaches at Dieppe can throw you off balance. The angle at which they slope into the water is both steep and dangerous. At high tide you can slide into the waves and lose your footing before you've remembered how to swim. The stones are treacherous. But they are also beautiful.

My father's ashes were contraband. You can't just walk about with someone's remains, in whatever form, in your suitcase. Stepping off the *Sealink* ferry, I carried my father in an envelope addressed to myself in Canada. This was only in case I was challenged. There was hardly more than a handful of him there. I had thrown the rest of him into the English Channel as the coast of Normandy was coming into view. It had been somewhat more than disconcerting to see the interest his ashes caused amongst the gulls and other sea birds. I had hoped to dispose of him in a private way, unnoticed. But a woman with two small children came and stood beside me at the railing and I heard her explain that *this nice gentleman is taking care of our feathered friends.* I hoped that, if my father was watching, he could laugh. I had to look away.

The ferry arrived in the early afternoon and — once I had booked myself into La Présidence Hotel — I went for a walk along the promenade above the sea-wall. It being May, the offshore breeze was warm and filled with the faintest scent of apple trees in bloom.

I didn't want to relive the battle. I hadn't come to conjure ghosts. But the ghosts and the battle are palpable around you there, no matter what your wishes are. The sound of the tide rolling back across the stones is all the cue you need to be reminded of that summer day in 1942. I stood that evening, resting my arms along the wall and thinking *at last, my father has come ashore.*

In the morning, before the town awoke, I got up in the dark and was on the beach when the sun rose inland beyond the cliffs. I wore a thick woollen sweater, walking shorts and a pair of running shoes. The envelope was in my pocket.

The concierge must have thought I was just another crazy North American off on my morning run. He grunted as I passed and I pretended not to know that he was there. Out on the beach, I clambered over retaining walls and petrified driftwood until I felt I was safely beyond the range of prying eyes.

The stones at Dieppe are mostly flint — and their colours range from white through yellow to red. The red stones look as if they have been washed in blood and the sight of them takes your breath away. I hunkered down above them, holding all that remained of my father in my fist. He felt like a powdered stone — pummelled and broken.

I let him down between my fingers, feeling him turn to paste — watching him divide and disappear.

He is dead and he is gone.

Weekends, our parents used to take us walking under the trees on Crescent Road. This was on the Rosedale side of Yonge Street. My brother Cy and I were always dressed in dark blue suits whose rough wool shorts would chafe against our thighs. Our knee socks — also blue — were turned down over thick elastic garters. Everything itched and smelled of Sunday. Cy had cleats on his shoes because he walked in such a way as to wear his heels *to the bone*, as my mother said — and causing much expense. The cleats made a wondrous clicking noise and you could always hear him coming. I wanted cleats, but I was refused because, no matter how I tried, I couldn't walk like that.

The houses sat up neat as pins beyond their lawns — blank-eyed windows, steaming chimneys — havens of wealth and all the mysteries of wealth.

Father often walked behind us. I don't know why. Mother walked in front with Rita. Rita always wore a dress that was either red or blue beneath her princess coat and in the wintertime she wore a sort of woollen cloche that was tied with a knitted string beneath her chin. Her Mary Jane shoes were just like Shirley Temple's shoes — which, for a while, was pleasing to Rita; then it was not. Rita always had an overpowering sense of image.

After the advent of our father's return, she said from the corner of her mouth one Sunday as we walked on Crescent Road that she and Cy and I had been named as if we were manufactured products: *Cy Max Office Equipment; Rita Max Household Appliances* and *Ben Max Watches*. This, she concluded, was why our father had always walked behind us. Proudly, he was measuring our performance. Now, he had ceased to walk behind us and our mother led us forward dressed in black.

Tick. Tick. Tick. That's me. The Ben Max Watch.

I have told our story. But I think it best — and I like it best — to end with all of us moving there beneath the trees in the years before the war. Mister and Mrs David Max out walking with their children any Sunday afternoon in any kind of weather but the rain.

Colonel Matheson, striding down his walk, is caught and forced to grunt acknowledgment that we are there. He cannot ignore us, after all. We have seen him every weekday morning, choosing his boutonnière and buying it from us.